STORIES RULE PRESS PRESENTS

2021 CHRISTMAS ROMANCE DIGEST

Home For The Holidays

EDITED BY TRACY COOPER-POSEY

STORIES RULE
EDMONTON • ALBERTA

Published by Stories Rule Press Inc.
Edmonton, Alberta, Canada.

Registered offices:
1100-10020 101A Avenue NW
Edmonton AB T5J 3G2

Edited by Tracy Cooper-Posey
Text design by Tracy Cooper-Posey

Print Layout by Cask & Sabre Publishing Consultancy

FIRST EDITION: October 2021

Romance—Fiction

Draft2Digital Print ISBN: 9781774384404

About Home For The Holidays

Heart-rending, happy-ending romances
to enhance your holidays!

Family get-togethers for the holiday season can sooth our emotions or savage our souls. No one knows us better than the family and friends we choose to share such times with.

In each of these seven delightful short romances, our heroes and heroines find going home for this season even more of a heart-wrench, for true love challenges their deepest held beliefs.

Going home for the holidays has never felt so wonderful.

This is the first annual edition of the Christmas Romance Digest, edited by national award-winning, best-selling romance author Tracy Cooper-Posey, featuring some of Romanceland's most beloved authors.

"A Christmas Carole" — Roxy Boroughs
"Just In Time For Christmas" — Lea Storry
"Because Of The Christmas Stroll" — Debbie Mumford
"The Invitation" — Jasmine Luck
"The Ghosts of Christmas Present" — Karen McCullough
"The Reunion" — Annie Reed
"Burying His Ghost of Christmas Past" — Tracy Cooper-Posey

Contemporary Short Romance Anthology

"Christmas Won't be Christmas Without Any Presents"

I first read Jo March's grumble, the opening line of *Little Women* by Louisa May Alcott, when I was very young—no more than ten years old. The book was a Christmas gift, a cheap hard cover edition that stayed on my bookshelves for decades, until I was forced to sell all my books to fund my migration to Canada.

And thus began my fascination with northern Christmas traditions and that creature which shuns Australian summers: The white Christmas. When I arrived in Canada in 1996, I was introduced to a real white Christmas less than three months later. I've loved snow and winter ever since.

One must experience a northern Christmas to understand so much about the tales and scenes we grow up with, even in the southern hemisphere. Until I moved to Canada, I had not tasted egg nog, even though I'd read about it for many years. I'm still learning the intricacies and fun of Christmas stockings. The very traditional oranges in stockings I did not fully understand until I'd survived a winter when fresh fruit is imported, and therefore expensive and hard to get.

However, Christmas is a world-wide event. Families and friends celebrate Christmas on every continent, including the Antarctic, where research and exploration crews take advantage of the mild summer days.

For that reason, I am very pleased to present this year's Christmas Romance anthology, which includes stories set not just in North America, but also in the United Kingdom and, of course, Australia. They are all lovely tales, filled with heart and warmth, and they stroll from quirky, to funny, to just a little dark and sad.

Consider this my Christmas present to you.

Enjoy.

Tracy Cooper-Posey
Edmonton, Alberta
October 2021

A Christmas Carole

Roxy Boroughs

"Santa...eloped?"

Carole Murray gulped. What about Mrs. Claus? When did she and Santa divorce? And who wound up with custody of the elves?

Man, she was losing it. Why fret about fictional dramas at the North Pole when she had real-life problems to worry about? Big ones.

Carole tightened her grip on the phone.

She was already short-staffed. One sales associate had come down with tonsillitis, while another broke his leg skiing. Could anything else go wrong this Christmas season?

As the manager of Baldwin's Department Store in Montpelier, Vermont, it was Carole's responsibility to turn a profit, to bring customers in the front door and make sure they kept coming back.

So, this December, she'd cooked up the idea to host a special guest—Santa Claus, himself.

She'd gone through a talent agency in the larger city of Burlington and hired a professional Santa to play the part. The older gentleman was an actual graduate of the Santa University in Colorado. Who knew such a place existed? He'd pose for photos with the kiddies, while the store absorbed the costs. A treat for their customers and the community.

Traditionally, Santa had an elf by his side to greet the kids and snap their photos. Mindful of her budget, Carole undertook the role of photographer and prepared to make her acting debut as said elf, in a costume she'd created on her late mother's sewing machine.

Santa, however, had eloped.

Carole took a deep breath and battened down her rising anxiety.

"An unforeseeable glitch," the talent agent concluded on the other end of the phone. "I'll send someone to replace him, immediately."

Good news, at last. But Carole had handpicked the original actor from resume photos, videos of him in the role and an interview via Zoom. He'd impressed her with his vast knowledge of the latest toys and gadgets, punctuating their chat with his perfect Santa laugh and a twinkle in his blue eyes.

"I just hope the new actor can get here in time." Carole glanced at her watch. Only twenty minutes before their scheduled start.

"Don't worry. He'll be there pronto. Guaranteed."

Carole voiced her thanks, wished the agent a Merry Christmas, and ended the call, not entirely reassured. With nervous energy to spare, she double-checked the preparations for Santa's visit. She didn't need any other surprises. Especially, with the store under new ownership.

Since high school, she'd worked for the Baldwin family, who'd owned the business for generations—one of the last independent department stores in the state. Now, at twenty-six, she was the youngest manager in the history of Baldwin's.

She didn't begrudge the past owners for wanting to retire. Neither of their adult children was interested in running the store, and Carole sure didn't have the funds to buy the business for what it was worth.

The Baldwins hoped Carole would stay on in her position, as would all the staff, but Carole wasn't taking any chances. R. J. Richman was notorious for gobbling up existing businesses, which he then revamped with an entirely new staff. Carole needed stellar sales figures this Christmas to secure everyone's job—sales she hoped her Santa idea would deliver.

She stopped by the front counters and received a ready smile from her head cashier, Shirley, who wore her customary black pants paired with the company's red shirt with the store's logo on the breast pocket. The color brought out Shirley's rosy cheeks and gray eyes. The pretty blonde, in her early fifties, bagged a young mom's purchases and gave each of the accompanying two children a sticker.

Shirley had come to work at Baldwin's three years ago, after her husband passed. "At first, I had to force a smile on my face for the customers," she'd once told Carole. "After a while, I didn't have to fake it anymore. Best therapy ever." And she'd been particularly perky in the last six months. Efficient, upbeat and endlessly patient, Shirley was loved by the customers and staff alike. Quickly, Carole explained the new Santa situation to her.

"Don't worry. If he's delayed, *I'll* wear the red suit."

In her antler headband, Shirley looked more like Blitzen than Santa, but Carole appreciated her cashier's zeal and grinned. "Thanks, Shirl. When the replacement arrives, please send him to me. You know where I'll be."

"Will do."

Carole continued her trek to the back of the store, where she'd set up Santa's area. Christmas music accompanied her, the latest pop tunes by the latest pop artists, available for download on the many devices in the electronics section. The mouth-watering scent of gingerbread circulated through the air, spread by diffusers, also sold in the store. Carole ensured actual gingerbread house kits were displayed nearby. She expected them to fly off the shelf.

At Santa's station, three sparkling artificial Christmas trees—one silver, one blue, and one green—surrounded a wide chair. Her dad, a semi-retired electrician, entertained himself with woodworking in his garage and had whipped up the green upholstered gold-trimmed throne, all from scraps.

To either side of the throne stood hip-high plastic candy canes filled with red, green and white popcorn. Like the Christmas trees, the candy canes were in stock and ready for purchase.

Finally, beside the chair sat a bag of small wooden toys, also crafted by her dad. He'd spent all year making them so they'd have enough to provide each child with a token present. On top of the pile, Carole spied a little duck on wheels, a car, a long-necked dinosaur, two whistles and a miniature unicorn.

"Excuse me. Are you the manager?"

At the mention of her title, Carole looked up to find a handsome stranger. She'd met many attractive men over the years, but the sight of this one sent a pleasant warmth over her skin. "Yes. Can I help you?"

"I was told to find you."

The new Santa. Though he'd arrived in record time, he sure didn't look the part. The guy could have been a Hollywood action hero. This thirty-something Adonis was well over six feet tall, tanned and toned, with wavy dark hair and a strong jaw. Not a local, surely. Carole would have remembered this man. Still, there was something familiar about his chocolate brown eyes.

"I'm so glad you're here. I'm Carole Murray. And you are?"

He hesitated.

How difficult a question was it?

"Robby," he said, at last.

Carole blinked, equally bewildered by his hesitancy and his answer. She'd known a Robby in high school, but this couldn't be the same person. He looked completely different from the boy in her memories. "Nice to meet you, Robby. You're a lifesaver."

His hand dwarfed hers when she shook it, a touch that spread tingles up her arm.

Customers first, she told herself. *Tingles later.*

She shied away from his animal attraction and hoped the beard and costume would conceal those linebacker shoulders. For her sake, as well as the character's. With a quick march, she led him to her office to change.

●

Which was how R. J. Richman, the new owner of Baldwin's Department Store, found himself in Carole's office with a Santa suit.

The windowless room was smaller than his walk-in closet, but better organized, with a whiteboard calendar on the wall above the desk. The word 'Santa' appeared in the boxes throughout the month, starting with today's date.

He eyed the costume on the hanger. "What have I gotten myself into?"

Carole obviously had him confused with someone who'd planned to dress up as the guy from the North Pole throughout December. R. J. had been about to explain her mistake, but she'd exited the room so fast he didn't get the chance.

Maybe the misunderstanding would work in his favor. Playing along with whatever Carole had planned meant he could get a look at the store's operations firsthand.

He stripped off his tie, jacket and dress shirt, shrugged on the provided undershirt and strapped on the Santa belly. The extra girth around his middle brought back all his teenage angst.

His parents' marriage hadn't been a happy one. While they argued, R. J. comforted himself with double helpings of burgers, fries and pizza. In those days, he'd gone by his birthname—Robby McFate. But the kids soon called him something else. Something that made him die a little inside every time he heard it.

Blobby McFat.

He'd cut classes to avoid the taunts. Studied on his own in the school library to keep up his grades. But even there, cocooned in the quiet shelter of books, breathing in their comforting smell, he wasn't safe. One day he remembered in particular, a group of bullies knocked the binder from his hands. The rings came undone and his notes flew into the air and spilled all over the carpeted floor.

He'd crouched to pick up the papers and felt a presence at his side. He turned, startled to see a pretty girl bent beside him, her dark hair held back in a clip, her luminous green eyes gazing at him.

"Hi. I'm Carole. Carole Murray. You're Robby, right?"

He'd braced himself, sure she'd follow with his nickname. But she hadn't. She'd helped him gather his notes and organize them back in his binder. They spent the rest of the period studying together and chatting. He was a few years older, a couple of grades ahead and able to explain the ins and outs of algebra to her.

He ran into her again the next day. And the day after. For weeks they met in the library. Found they enjoyed the same books, the same

TV shows. Soon, Robby felt like he could talk to her about anything, even his parents' crumbling marriage. She never judged him, never made fun of his appearance.

They began walking home together. Occasionally, his hand would accidentally brush hers, making his heart beat faster. The last day of school, he worked up the nerve to kiss her—a kiss he still remembered. Soft, sweet, minty—the closest thing to heaven he'd experienced.

The next day, his folks' divorce came through and his mom took him to live in California. There, he vowed to change his life. Start over. He ate more vegetables, which helped clear up his acne. He joined a gym and worked out regularly. Later, when he began earning his own money, he elected for LASIK eye surgery, which allowed him to ditch his thick glasses.

He'd even changed his name to R. J. Richman. *Mister* Richman to his employees. He had no intention of going back to the Robby of old. He despised that guy and had no idea why he'd introduced himself that way to Carole.

No. That wasn't entirely true. Seeing her again, after all these years—appreciating how the pretty girl from his youth had become an extraordinarily beautiful woman—it had momentarily dazed him. And a small part of him wanted to know if she'd remembered him. Though he wasn't surprised she hadn't recognized him. He was a new man now. A successful one.

After launching his flagship Richman's store in San Francisco and scoring his first million, he'd made it his goal to put his competition out of business. Or buy them up and turn the establishment into another jewel in his empire.

With his healthy bank account and healthy body weight, women flocked to him with the same passion they'd once used to avoid him. At first, he reveled in his newfound popularity. Took advantage of it. Until he realized just how shallow the ladies were. And how shallow he'd become.

Through it all, his memories came back to Carole. She'd liked him despite his appearance. She'd liked him…well…for him.

R. J. chucked his trousers and stepped into Santa's red pants with the fur trim. The black boots were a little tight but he'd tough it out. He plucked a tissue from the box on Carole's desk and used it to clean up a scuff mark on the left heel.

And, speaking of heels, he was starting to feel like one.

He should have cleared up Carole's mistake right away too. But the electric jolt of seeing her again made him unable to trust himself to speak, worried his voice might crack as it had when he was an adolescent.

He should have explained the purpose of his visit. Sure, he wanted to tour the store in person, but when he'd seen Carole's name listed as manager, he knew he had to see her again. Was it foolish to wonder if she'd loved him then? Even a little bit? Was it stupid to hope she might fall in love with him now?

She still went by the same last name. Did that mean she was single? That he hadn't waited too long to return home triumphantly?

He donned the mustache and beard and topped it off with the Santa hat. The white pompom dangled near his cheekbone.

What am I doing? As the new owner, he couldn't go parading around as Santa. *Where's your dignity, man?* More to the point, Carole had already failed to recognize him in his business suit. She'd never guess who he was in this getup. And he wanted her to know. Wanted to reconnect with her.

R. J. was about to peel off his disguise when a knock sounded at the door.

Carole poked her head into the room. "Ready?"

She entered and the office shrank. Not that he'd complain. The limited space allowed him to admire the rest of her and how adorable she looked in her elf costume. Green suited her—matched her sparkling eyes and accentuated the deep brown of her wavy hair.

R. J. liked her tights too, which showed off long, toned legs.

He cleared his throat. "Almost," he replied, in answer to her question. "What now?"

Her brows shot upward. "Didn't the agency explain it to you?"

Here was his chance to resolve the confusion. Instead, out of his mouth sprang a single word. "No."

She sighed. "It's pretty straightforward. The usual Santa shtick."

"Shtick?" R. J. hadn't thought about Santa in years. Gave up hoping for his Christmas wishes to come true when he was five. He wracked his brain trying to remember Santa's routine.

"You know. 'Ho-ho-ho,' and wish everyone a Merry Christmas. That's what it's about—spreading cheer and making people happy. Let the kids sit on your knee and ask them what they want you to bring them. But remember, don't make any promises."

That made sense. Who knew what they'd actually get on Christmas morning? Couldn't have Santa vow to bring a much wanted toy, then forget. It would spoil the fantasy.

"Afterward, if the parents want, you'll pose with their kids for a photo."

Like a mall Santa, R. J. surmised. He didn't have a lot of experience with children—none, in fact—but imagined it wouldn't be too hard for him to pull off. "How much are we charging for the photos?"

"Nothing."

"Nothing?!" He nearly choked on the word. "This is a commercial business. It's here to make a profit...." He trailed off when a heated flush crept into her cheeks.

"That's the plan. You'll also be passing out little wooden toys."

"Toys too? How much is this costing—" He almost added 'me,' but caught himself in time.

Carole's eyes narrowed. "Don't worry. You'll be paid regardless. But I figure we'll more than make up the expense. People will be in a good mood and, since they're already here, they'll shop. After the kids speak to you, their parents will know exactly what to buy."

Finally, a strategy R. J. could get behind. As for his hopes to rekindle his relationship with Carole, her pursed lips, as kissable as they were, suggested he wasn't anywhere near to closing that deal.

●

Carole had no idea performers were so inquisitive. Why did her promotional budget matter to this Robby fellow? Maybe the guy was a method actor and needed the details to create his character. He was an experienced Santa, after all. Carole couldn't imagine the talent agency would send her a novice.

But his name...now that was a coincidence.

She'd known a Robby in high school—Robby McFate. They'd spent a lot of time together, shared their thoughts, even revealed their middle names to one another. Jackson for him, Ann for her. Carole thought hers pretty plain, so he'd christened her with a pet name.

Carillon.

"Because your laugh sounds like tinkling bells," he'd told her.

She'd looked up the word. Found there was a carillon in Middlebury—a tower with twenty-three ringing bells that played tunes, operated from a keyboard which looked like the pedals of a big church organ. At this time of year, she imagined it would play Christmas music, which always made her smile.

She remembered her walks home from school with Robby. How, on the last day of classes, he'd kissed her—a sweet kiss which made her heart flutter and her stomach do a flip-flop. Even thinking about it now, heat spread over her cheeks and butterflies flapped in her belly.

She'd been kissed since, of course. But nothing compared to that first heart-stopping, soul-baring kiss she'd shared with Robby.

Soon after, he'd moved away without a word. He never contacted her later and, when she'd searched for him online, it was as if he'd fallen off the edge of the planet. No Facebook account. No Instagram. Nothing.

This man couldn't be the same guy. He looked so different. Especially with a curly white synthetic beard.

Still, those brown eyes...

She remembered Robby's. His were sad, except when they were together. She knew he was teased in school and, though he was shy and rarely spoke to other students, when he did speak, he was always thoughtful and articulate.

Whatever happened to him?

She shrugged off the question, lifted the Santa jacket from the hanger and held it out for the Robby currently in her company. He turned his back to her and slipped his arms in the sleeves. Carole ran her palms over the fabric, hand-ironing it—an excuse to feel the solid muscles over those big, broad shoulders.

Stop it, she ordered herself. In her elf role, she couldn't crush over Santa. How would that look?

Jacket on, Robby fastened the wide black belt around his expanded waist, perched Santa's signature gold-rimmed glasses on his nose and was ready to go. She led him out of her office and into the store area. From a distance, she could see people already in line behind the velvet rope she'd set up.

"You can start any time," she instructed quietly, as they approached the crowd.

"Start?"

"You know, being Santa. Ho-ho-ho-ing and stuff."

"Oh, right." He slapped a hand onto his padded belly. "Ho-ho-ho."

His laugh didn't quite achieve that deep resonance she expected. "Lower I think."

He bent at the knees, which knocked his height down a foot. "Ho-ho-ho."

Carole did a double-take. Did he just make a joke? A visual one, at that?

"Sorry. Couldn't resist." He straightened and tried the laugh at a lower register. "Ho-ho-ho."

"Much better."

The guy even had a sense of humor like Robby's. He'd made her laugh then and this man made her laugh now. It broke the ice. He seemed a little less stiff in his role and waved to the waiting kids as he took his seat.

Carole welcomed the first child in line. The red-headed girl, bundled up in a pretty blue coat with faux fur trim, scampered up and plunked herself on Santa's lap, her long braids flying.

"Hello." Robby added another 'ho-ho,' to rhyme with his greeting.

"And what would you like for Christmas?"

"You're supposed to ask my name first. Otherwise, you won't know where to bring my present."

Robby's lips quirked into a grin. "Sorry about that. I'm a little tired after driving in from the North Pole on my sleigh."

Carole hid a chuckle behind her camera. The child's parents laughed too.

"So," Robby continued. "What's your name, little girl?"

"I'm Dora. Like the Explorer."

"Nice name."

"I hate it."

Robby peered at the girl over his spectacles. "Totally understand that. Felt the same way when I was your age. Did you want me to bring you a new name for Christmas?"

"No, silly Santa. I want a jewelry-making kit, so I can design rings and bracelets with pretty beads."

"Ah, you're crafty."

The kid crossed her arms and harumphed. "No, I told you, I'm Dora."

"Yes, yes. Don't worry, Dora. I won't forget."

With the permission of the girl's parents, Carole snapped a photo of Dora, as Robby presented her with a wooden unicorn. "You can pick up the print at the photocenter, with our compliments," Carole told the family. "Merry Christmas."

She and Robby fell into a comfortable rhythm—her welcoming the kids, him listening to their Christmas wishes, and her capturing the joyous moment on camera.

Shirley, on a break, appeared with her two grandchildren—aged five and seven. Shirley held onto the girls' winter coats so they could show off their matching A-line dresses—red on top but flared out to reveal a snow-covered image of the North Pole along the bottom.

Carole dropped to one knee so she could talk to Emma and Olivia face to face. "Don't you ladies look lovely!"

They beamed and Emma, the older of the two and more outgoing, twirled around like a model.

"Are you ready to meet Santa?"

Emma nodded, but Olivia pulled back and held onto her sister's hand for dear life.

"There's nothing to worry about," Carole assured them. "Santa won't bite." To prove it, she tickled Robby under his beard and was startled when he let out a bark.

"Arf!"

She snapped back her hand and turned to the kids, sure he'd frightened them, but the two girls laughed uproariously.

Olivia's shyness evaporated and she skipped up to Santa and plopped herself down on his knee without any more coaxing.

This Robby certainly wasn't a conventional Santa, but he amused and charmed the parents and children alike. After posing for pictures with Emma and Olivia, he distracted one screaming toddler with a wooden dinosaur, and didn't fuss when another wet herself while seated on his lap.

Though his eyes weren't blue like the Santas Carole had come to expect, those brown ones of his did crinkle at the corners and sparkle with humor and intelligence. She made a mental note to call the talent agent at the end of the day and commend Robby's performance.

Carole spotted her receiver, Leroy, next in line with his little boy—a curly-headed eight-year-old with big hazel eyes, his Christmas tree bowtie peeking out between his scarf and his zippered jacket. "Hello, Jamal. I see you brought your daddy with you. He's a very important man around here. We couldn't run the store without him."

Leroy unloaded and tracked the merchandise as it came in, and helped place it on the shelves. If the stock wasn't properly accounted for, the store could be out thousands, even millions of dollars.

Carole ushered Jamal over to Robby, who lifted the boy onto his knee. The dry one.

"And what do you want for Christmas, Jamal?" Santa asked with another, "Ho-ho-ho."

A line appeared between the little boy's brows. "I want my daddy to keep his job."

•

R. J. jolted. Why would Jamal ask him that? It was as if the kid had read his mind.

Whenever R. J. bought a business, pink slips followed. He supposed he could hire some of the store's employees back at a reduced rate, but found those who returned under such conditions did so with a negative attitude. Better to start over with new staff, at a lower hourly wage and train them to his own satisfaction.

He'd overheard Jamal's conversation with Carole and knew his father worked in the store. He'd seen Leroy's name on the payroll sheets and had already drafted the man's dismissal.

"Sorry. That's something I can't guarantee, Jamal."

Carole's head whipped around at R. J.'s statement. "But Santa is going to work really hard on that, right, Santa?" she asked, ignoring her earlier advice about promises. She didn't wait for his reply, but barreled on. "Now, Jamal, is there something else you'd like? A toy, perhaps?"

"Nope. I just want to help my dad. He's worried about the take up."

"Take *over*," R. J. corrected and Carole shot him another pointed look.

She retrieved a BE BACK IN TEN MINUTES sign and looped it over the curved end of one candy cane.

"We're taking a quick break, folks…to feed the reindeer," she announced.

She jerked her head, a clear indication for R. J. to follow her.

When he stood, she linked her arm with his and propelled him to her office with more force than he would have guessed she possessed, given her petite size.

As soon as she closed the door, she whirled on her heel. "What in sleigh bell's name are you doing?"

"You said not to make promises."

Her gaze, hot as pokers, bore into him and he started sweating under his fake hair and beard. "Kids are never too young to deal with the reality of life," he added.

"From Santa?" Carole huffed. "I'll tell you about reality, mister. Jamal's mother drained the family bank account and took off with another man. Leroy is a good father and a good person. He didn't deserve that. Neither did Jamal."

R. J. winced. His own father had left his mom for another, younger woman. His mother had done her best to raise him while holding down two jobs. From that experience, he'd vowed never to be poor again. *Business is business.* That's what he'd always told himself, while ignoring the harm he might do to others with his new philosophy.

"Leroy has worked for Baldwin's most of his life," she went on. "As have I. We love this store. We respect the employees who make it run and the customers who've supported the business since its beginning. That doesn't make us blind to reality. We understand the store has to make a profit. We do it by creating a workplace that operates for everyone."

Robby wasn't surprised by Carole's point of view. He'd noticed that she knew many of the people who'd lined up to see Santa and greeted them by name. Not just her colleagues and their children, but customers too. She'd always shown an interest in people. Always had a caring personality.

Under her sharp gaze, Robby cooked in his costume. He tore off his hat and wig. They landed on her desk, his fake beard following.

Fake. The perfect description for him. No matter how much weight he'd lost, or how much money he'd earned, he couldn't escape his past. His chin sank to his chest. "Oh, Carillon."

"*Robby?* Robby McFate?"

He'd said the nickname he'd given her without thinking. Now, there was no turning back. He met her eye, unsure how to answer. He hadn't used his real name in years. And yet, right now, at this minute, that's exactly who he was. *Blobby McFat.*

"It *is* you, isn't it?"

He swallowed. "Yes." He didn't know what to expect from her

now. Disappointment? Surprise?

She stood still for a moment, her eyes big, her mouth opened in shock. Tentatively, she took a step toward him, which left them chest to chest in the small space.

He wasn't sure who initiated the embrace. Was it him? Her? Maybe it was an unspoken and mutual attraction, like a couple of magnets drawn together by nature. A second later, he lost his ability to think, because she was in his arms, her body pressed close. As close as possible with his Santa belly between them. He wanted to ditch it so he could hold her tighter, but didn't want to break away from her for the time it would take to shed it.

"Robby. Oh, Robby. It's so good to see you."

"You too." And to feel her. Hear her velvety voice whisper in his ear. Smell her floral perfume, warm and feminine.

His lips strayed to her cheek. His mouth sought hers, picking up on that kiss they'd shared so long ago as if only seconds had passed between them. He'd loved her back then and that had never faded. He loved her still.

When they came up for air, her skin was flushed, her lips swollen.

"Robby.... I've dreamed of seeing you again. Of getting another shot at that kiss. You took me by surprise that first time. This time too."

"I've developed a few more skills since then."

"Have you ever."

He laughed, happy she'd enjoyed the kiss as much as he had.

She stepped back, holding his hands, and sighed. "You might think this strange, but I always thought fate had brought us together. Just like your name. I looked for you on the internet and never found a Robby McFate."

"My mom remarried and her new husband adopted me. Insisted I take his last name." And R. J. hadn't minded in the least.

"But...what are you doing here, pretending to be Santa?"

How could he answer? He didn't understand it himself. Santa was supposed to bring gifts, while he intended to put a lump of coal in his employees' stockings.

Maybe a few lumps for the community too.

He frowned. Usually, R. J. avoided one-on-one confrontations. It was far easier to fire people on paper than in person. But he'd looked forward to coming home. Wanted to flaunt his achievements in front of all the bullies who'd once mocked him.

He couldn't change his nature. Anymore than Carole could change hers. She was naturally personable. Caring. A pushover, some might say. None of those qualities put cash in the bank.

"I'm R. J. Richman, the new owner. And once the holidays are done, I'm taking over."

●

Soon after, Carole's real hired Santa made his appearance, already dressed in his own costume.

And Robby? He'd changed into his suit and hung around the store for a while, then disappeared without saying goodbye.

Now, four weeks later, on Christmas Eve, Carole sat in her apartment over the garage of her dad's house, not sure she had a job to return to after the holidays.

She paced for a bit, sat on the couch again, had a shower, put on clean sweatpants and a comfy old sweater, then paced some more.

She couldn't believe Robby had come back to town. *And* looked completely different from when he'd left.

No. Not Robby. He was R. J. Richman now. She doubted her job would survive the take-over, especially after the dressing-down she'd given him.

She rubbed her eyes with the heels of her hands. Why had she opened her big mouth? R. J. Richman was well known for firing everyone and starting fresh with new hires. She'd hoped that with great sales, she could change that inevitable conclusion. But her hopes fell, just like the snow outside her window.

Generally, she liked to see those soft flakes falling on the huge maple tree in the yard, its leaves bursting with reds and oranges during the fall, but now stripped and naked. Much like she felt.

The bleakness outside her window matched the bleakness in her heart. The five-foot high Christmas tree in the corner of her living room had looked festive when she'd first decorated it. Now, its flashing lights and tinsel mocked her with its merriness.

She'd opened herself up to Robby. Confessed her feelings with a kiss, not realizing who he really was. Or rather, who he'd become.

She remembered her head cashier's words. Shirley had picked herself up after the loss of her husband. She'd faked enthusiasm at first, until it became a habit.

Time for Carole to follow suit. She grabbed the latest newspaper to peruse the Wanted ads, pen in hand, though she knew retail work would be scarce after the holidays. Businesses did their best to hold onto their profits by reducing staff hours.

A rap on the door brought her head up. Her dad let himself in and closed the door, then shed his boots and coat to reveal his work jeans and a blue plaid shirt. "How are you doing, honey?"

"Hanging in."

She put the paper to one side and he sat beside her, hands clasped. "Losing your job isn't such a bad thing, Carole. If that's what happens. Now you can go anywhere, do anything. Follow those dreams you left behind."

"Left behind?"

"I know you've stayed here because of me."

She'd had her own place for a few years but, after her mom died, she'd wanted to be near her father. To keep him company and help out with some cooking. Though, honestly, he made far more suppers for her than she did for him.

Her tiny apartment had everything she needed. Its open concept featured a main room with a cozy kitchen and enough space for a couch and TV. One door led to a separate area for sleeping. A second hid a compact bathroom. The walls, painted as white as Santa's beard, made the apartment look bigger and brighter than it truly was, and provided the perfect backdrop for the photos and wall accents she'd picked up over the years. Though homey, it wasn't exactly the home she'd envisioned for herself, but she couldn't complain. It was a practical solution that afforded her some privacy, while living close to her father.

"I love you, Dad. And I love…*loved* my job. Loved working for the Baldwins."

"There's so much more waiting for you out there in the world. It's waiting for me too."

She swiveled to face him. "What do you mean, Dad?"

He took a deep breath. "I've met someone."

Carole scooped her jaw off the floor. He'd never mentioned a word about dating, though she certainly had no objections. He was an adult and free to live his life. Whatever made him happy was fine with her.

"When?"

"I've known her for years, but our relationship turned romantic six months ago."

Six months? Carole couldn't believe he'd kept it a secret that long. If she hadn't been so busy at the store, she might have noticed the signs—the renewed spring in his step and how he'd suddenly become a fabulous cook.

"So those dinners I thought you made—"

"We made them together. I never knew cooking could be so much fun."

Fun and delicious. Carole could attest to the yumminess of their culinary adventures.

Remembering last week's creamy mac and cheese with fiddleheads on the side, and tart apple pie for dessert, made her mouth water all over again. "I'm happy for you. Truly. I'm just surprised you didn't tell me."

He hunched his shoulders. "I worried you'd think I didn't love your mom. And I did. I do. But I miss female companionship. I miss talking to someone my own age, who has similar life experiences."

That made sense. The most natural thing in the world. "I understand, Dad. Of course, you want to share your life with someone."

She'd once thought Robby would be that person for her. That

they'd always be together. That they'd eventually marry and create a family of their own.

Carole grabbed one of the throw cushions and held it close, wishing she could hold onto her dreams of happiness with him. But they'd never be a couple. Not now.

Still, she wouldn't let her own disappointment mar her father's good news. He'd found that special relationship twice in a lifetime. First, with her mom, and now with this mystery woman.

"If you want my blessing, Dad, you've got it. When do I get to meet her?"

He blushed. "Actually, you've already met. It's someone you know. Quite well, in fact."

"Who?"

"It's Shirley."

Carole clapped a hand to her chest. "Shirley? *My* Shirley?"

"Guess she's *our* Shirley now. That's okay with you, isn't it?"

Love was in the air. The first Santa she'd hired had eloped and now her dad and Shirley were an item. Too bad things hadn't worked out between her and Robby.

She tossed the pillow onto the floor, shifted closer to her father and looped her arm in his. "It's more than okay. It's terrific. For both you and Shirley. She found a good catch."

"Me too. It means you don't have to worry about me. You can live your own life."

Right when it was falling apart.

"By the way, Shirley's son is home from Texas for the holidays. She's planning a big Christmas dinner tomorrow with him, her daughter, her grandkids...and us. Shirley wants us all to be together to celebrate as a family."

Shirley's cooking was enough to entice Carole. Being part of an extended family put the proverbial cherry on top. "I'd love to go."

They confirmed the plans for tomorrow, Carole agreeing to bring wine and homemade shortbread cookies.

When her dad left, she set out her recipe book for the morning and went to bed, eager for Christmas Day to arrive. Santa wouldn't be bringing her true love this year, but celebrating with her father, Shirley and her family was the perfect distraction to see Carole through.

●

A pounding on the roof brought Carole out of a restless sleep. She glanced at the clock on her bedside table. *Midnight. Christmas Day.*

But what was the racket on the roof? It sounded like—dare she think it?—reindeer hooves.

"Ho-ho-ho."

She started at the voice, swept the covers off and shrugged on her housecoat. She flung open her front door and there he stood. Santa.

Well…really it was Robby, dressed as Santa.

"What are you doing here?" Besides letting cold air into her apartment. She rubbed one bare foot over the other to warm them.

"I'm spreading Christmas cheer."

Seriously? Carole threw her hands in the air and walked away. She heard the door shut, not sure which side of it he'd ended up on and not caring, either.

"I have a present for you."

So, he'd stayed. She turned and popped her fists onto her hips. Did he think he could soften the blow of dismissing her with a gift? Apparently, yes. And her treacherous heart agreed. It thumped around her chest, fueled by his presence, still hoping for the impossible.

"Does the present involve that noise on the roof?"

"I threw a few snowballs to wake you." He stomped the white stuff from his boots, slipped them off and left them on the shoe mat. "My actual present involves the Christmas sales figures."

Typical. This all came down to business. "And?"

"They're unbelievable. You doubled last year's gross and did better per square foot than my flagship store." He took a tentative step toward her. "I didn't think it was possible, but by spending a little money on your Santa idea, you exceeded my expectations."

Small praise. It didn't change anything. Not their relationship, or her job prospects.

His long strides ate up the short distance between them. "I'm going to repeat your program in all my stores next year, Carole. And I want you to be a part of it."

Her heart all but stopped. *"Me?"*

"You had the vision. The know-how."

She controlled herself. He was offering her a job, a definite turn of fortune. Was she a fool to want more? "What about my staff?"

R. J. removed his fake beard and hung his head. "When we reunited that day in the store, I may have worn a Santa suit, but I acted like Scrooge. Success was something I worked hard to get, then felt I had to parade it in front of everyone, avenging myself on a world that once made fun of me. I thought it would make me happy, but it didn't. The chip on my shoulder became a log, a whole forest. It was an empty existence." His eyes sought hers. "Seeing you with the staff, with the customers, that changed something deep inside me."

His sincerity melted her. "I'm glad." She reached up to touch his face, but thought better of it and stuffed the offending hand in the pocket of her bathrobe. "You still haven't told me your thoughts about the staff."

"I tried not to think about them at all. Tried to view them as names on a page. That made it easier to clean house. Sometimes, you have to make tough decisions in business. I'm sure you've had to fire employees."

"I've dismissed a few over the years." Mostly for poor job performance, though she'd caught one stealing. It was never easy, but sometimes necessary. "*You* usually fire *everyone.*"

"To save money. I would save on paper, but at what cost? After your real Santa arrived, I toured the store. Saw how well trained your staff is—people like Shirley and Leroy. I saw how they take pride in their work and I wondered how much money I'd lose hiring all new people."

He paced along the kitchen island, gesturing with his hands as he talked. "When an inexperienced cashier is struggling to find the right button to press, how many busy customers decide they can't wait and leave the store without making a purchase? Perhaps never to return? If new employees ticket the merchandise incorrectly, how much shrinkage is there, making price adjustments until the mistake is resolved? How many add-on purchases are lost because sales staff aren't familiar with the stock? Because they don't think to show a customer the matching towels that go with their new shower curtain? How much harder will an employee work when they're fairly incentivized with a reasonable hourly rate and the chance of receiving promotions? When they have a stake in the company?"

All good points, to Carole's mind. "Sounds like you've given this a great deal of thought."

"I have. You've helped me take a second look at my business. To realize people are a part of it. A big part. That's why I'm going to keep everyone on."

Her mouth gaped open. "Honestly?"

"Honestly. Why mess with success? But the deal only works if you're on board. What do you say?"

What could she say? She gave a leap for joy and cheered. "Yes. I say, yes."

"And to me? What do you say to me?"

Carole's breath caught. She tempered her expectations, afraid of misreading him, and making a fool of herself. "I don't understand."

"I think you do. I know we only spent a few hours together earlier this month. But we have a history. I hope it's not too late to admit that I had a huge crush on you. Still do. You saw past the acne and the glasses and the pounds."

"I never cared about those things. I cared about you, Robby. Or maybe I should call you R. J."

"With you, I'm Robby, again. A new and improved one, I hope… my sweet Carillon." He swept her into his arms. "I loved you then and I love you now."

He kissed her, deepened it, put his heart and soul into it, until her knees buckled. If he hadn't been holding her, she would have fallen into a heap at his feet.

"I'm not going to lie, Robby," she confessed, once she could form words. She ran her hand over his broad chest, relishing the feel of him. "I like this version of you too."

"My Santa version?"

She tickled him under his chin, just as she had in the store, only this time he didn't bite back. "You do look very cute in that costume."

"And I couldn't take my eyes off you in that elf outfit."

"It's hanging in my bedroom closet." She waggled her brows at him.

"That's quite the invitation. But you, on your own, are enough to satisfy me. No costumes, no role-playing. Just us." He sat on one of the island's barstools and drew her into his arms. His kiss warmed her in places she'd almost forgotten existed.

Turned out her dad wasn't the only one who'd found love twice in a lifetime. She had too, with her high school sweetheart. He'd been lost for a time, but he'd finally come home to her.

Hopefully, Shirley had room for one more dinner guest.

"Santa, baby," Carole drawled, as she snatched the red hat from Robby's head and tossed it onto the counter beside his fake beard. "You've made all my Christmas wishes come true."

"All of them?" His brown eyes twinkled.

"Well..." She nibbled on his earlobe. "Let's see what happens once that Santa suit comes off."

Before launching her writing career, the multi-talented Roxy Boroughs was an accomplished stage and film actor who appeared in the TV series *Degrassi Junior High*; and top-rated movies such as *It Must Be Love*, starring Ted Danson and Mary Steenburgen.

Look for her romantic comedy *Crazy for Cowboy*; her suspense series *Psychic Heat,* featuring the award-winning novel *A Stranger's Touch*; and the popular *Frost Family Christmas* series, marrying sweet romance with cozy mystery.

Visit Roxy's site: https://www.roxyboroughs.com/

Just in Time for Christmas

Lea Storry

"Stay," said my head.

"Go," said my heart.

So which one did I listen to?

The one that led me home to Harbour Blue for Christmas.

I have neither the time nor the...time to celebrate a holiday. Yet here I am. Isolating. Alone. Tons of work. In a snowstorm. With no food. And absolutely no caffeine. I had overlooked that part when planning my trip. Caffeine is how I power through my long days. Thankfully, I put in an order at the local, and only, small town grocery store this morning.

Honk, honk!

A horn blaring from a vehicle blasts a hole in my concentration. I look outside from my desk. All I can see are snowflakes. Many, many fat and clumsy snowflakes falling to the ground. I can't see the ocean, which is practically on my beautiful, two-story Victorian rental house's doorstep.

Honk, honk!

"What's their problem?" I mutter. "I don't have time for this."

I had decided, last minute, to leave Paris and visit my family on the east coast of Canada despite the 14-day quarantine required for anyone travelling here from out of the country. I could have stayed in Europe, worked over Christmas and toasted the New Year with a glass of champagne, solo, but I was craving the cheer and warmth of home. At forty-seven-years-old, I live a comfortable life but I'm just so far away from my parents and they're only getting older. I had arrived in Nova Scotia last night, December 10th. Today is my first full day in isolation and I'm already regretting it. I'm falling behind and the weight of my work is giving me a headache.

A couple more honks and I put on my fine cashmere pink coat and slip on my new grey suede leather boots. I bought the shoes in a store in my Paris neighbourhood last week. These boots will not hold up to the Maritime storm raging outside.

I open the heavy front door and am immediately pummeled by flying snow and a cold salty breeze. I shiver—and I'm not even outside yet. I try to lift my feet over the wet and deep white stuff, but it's no use. My boots disappear in the drifts, which are almost up to my knees. I wade to the eggshell blue gate a few metres away.

I can't see who is on the other side of the fence, but I can hear them huffing and puffing along with the grating of a shovel hitting concrete.

"What's going on?" I shout to the noise.

"I'm trying to deliver your items but your gate is stuck," a man calls back. "Too much snow packed in front of it."

"So?"

"Well, I thought you could open the gate from your end. But then I started digging. I'm almost finished."

"Then why do you need me?" Frustration edges my words. "I was working. Now my new boots are dead, thanks to you."

The gate is pushed slowly open to reveal a man with his hair coated with snow and friendly brown eyes above a green mask over his mouth and nose.

"Sorry about your boots, Tamzin," the stranger says.

"Do I know you?" I tuck a snow-coated curl behind my ear.

"Um, yeah." The man shakes his head and the snow falls off, revealing thick black hair. "Don't you recognize me?" he asks.

My headache is getting worse. I'm standing in the cold snow while more cold snow piles on top of my head. I feel like a snowperson in the North Pole.

"Are you Santa Claus?" I say, sarcastically. "Look, I simply want my coffee."

"I have all your caffeination supplies and I will also eat any cookies you leave out. Alas, I'm not Saint Nicholas, I'm Keiran Cho."

I gulp.

"You're Judy's younger brother. I haven't seen you in twenty-five years."

"Yep. I'd recognize you anywhere," Keiran says. "Same curly blonde hair and blue eyes."

"Judy and I are Facebook friends."

"She's married," Keiran says. "Couple of kids."

"I know."

"She said you're living in France? Working for a big engineering company?"

"Yes." I keep my answers brief, hoping Keiran will get the hint.

"Your order is in the vehicle. Just a second." Keiran scrambles through the snow to a green van with its windshield wipers working overtime.

The name of his family's store, Cho's Groceries, is written on the side in black. The man grabs several plastic bags and hauls them to me.

"I'll put these on the step," he says. "Health regulations say I'm not supposed to come into the house."

I pull the collar of my thin coat closer around my neck. It's letting snow and the damp East Coast humidity in.

Keiran strides through the snow like it's powdered sugar, not dense slush. I can't help noticing his broad shoulders in his navy-blue wool peacoat. He puts the bags down gently on the wooden veranda, after brushing off the snow that has accumulated on it.

"Thanks," I say, already thinking about how to handle this breach of my schedule.

"We're all about service at Cho's," Keiran says. "Well, more like what *I'm* all about. Not sure if you heard, but my Uppa died a few weeks ago."

Shoot! I had made that rude comment about my shoes being dead. "I'm so sorry about your father," I say. "I remember Mr. Cho well. He was always friendly and welcoming. I loved when Judy asked me to stay for supper at your house. He made the most delicious dumplings."

"He did! You'd eat all the mandu and I wouldn't get any. I didn't mind."

"You had no choice." I chuckle. "You were Judy's much younger and dorky brother."

Keiran laughs. Then he stares straight into my eyes. Something about the way he looks at me sends shivers down my spine and not because I'm cold.

"You know, Tamzin, it's great to see you," he says.

"You, too, Keiran."

"I've got to run. Other orders to fill and this nor'easter is forecasted to turn to freezing rain soon. I'll catch you later."

Keiran hops into his van, turns it around and heads down the road in a flurry of snow.

Keiran Cho. I haven't thought about him in years. He's got to be at least eight years younger than me. He had been a skinny little boy who wore his jeans hiked up to his armpits when I saw him last.

Now, Keiran is all grown up, while I had a tantrum like a child, over coffee and lost minutes.

"At least I'm consistent," I mutter.

It's exactly why Raul broke up with me, last year. If I'm not working, I'm working on working. I never give myself time to relax.

A gust of wind hits me in the face.

I need to get back to my desk. I close the gate and trudge to the porch, lug the groceries inside and then shake everything off, including me.

I unpack the coffee beans first. I need the hit of caffeine to push past my jetlag. The place I booked for the holidays has everything I would ever want: a bean grinder, fast and reliable internet and a large den complete with a desk. The ocean view simply comes with the house. The only thing I have time to look at is my computer screen.

With my instant meals put away and the coffee brewed, I fill a mug.

"Crap!" The store forgot to include milk with my order. Usually, it's my assistant, Andre, who handles everything and anything in my domestic realm. He has people who stock my kitchen, clean my apartment, do my laundry, cook my meals and buy my coffee so I can think of more important stuff than milk.

I could ask my Mom to bring some over, but I don't want her on the road in this crazy weather.

I sigh, pick up my phone and call the grocery store. "This is Tamzin Martins," I say when a woman answers. "Someone at the store forgot my milk."

"I'm sorry," the woman says. "Let me bring up your order."

I hear her tapping on a computer.

"Ms. Martins, there is no milk listed here. If you give us a couple of hours, we'll send you a litre. Does that work for you?"

"Fine."

I'd much rather a coffee with milk but caffeine is caffeine. I drink my black coffee absentmindedly, while I tackle the business of estimating how much time and money it'll cost to get a barge from France to Spain. My shoulders are creeping up to my ears and my head is aching like it has been stomped on by giants. As usual, I'm lost in problems and barely register the pain.

The doorbell rings, startling me. I look at the clock on my screen, it's almost five p.m. and getting dark. I hurry to the front door.

It's Keiran. I feel a tiny, unexplainable ember warm my stomach.

He takes a couple of steps back from me and shows me a jug of milk. *"Moooo."*

"Har, har."

He puts the milk down in front of him. "What were you doing?"

"Working," I say, rubbing my temples.

"Take a break?"

"What? Now? I have piles of things to do and it's only five."

"*Only* five? When do you log off?"

"Never." I glance back into the living room, where a large clock is counting down the seconds I'm away from my computer.

"It's almost bedtime for people in France," Keiran says. "Grab your coat and meet me out the back. I'm sure you have ten minutes."

"I wish I did." I begin to close the door on his friendly face.

"Hold on, hold on." Keiran puts up his hand. "Five minutes, then."

I look at the clock again. "Five minutes." I grab the milk and hustle inside. I stick the milk in the fridge, then put on my coat and ruined suede boots. "Why didn't I bring warmer clothing?" I ask myself. I'd known where I was heading. Harbour Blue is not only known for its quaint downtown with cute seaside shops and a tearoom that serves hot scones and tart jelly, but the town also gets hit with wicked winter storms that wreak havoc on power lines and bring the community to a standstill.

A fuzzy beige blanket tossed over the sofa offers to provide me with some warmth. I grab it.

I hadn't realized there was a back porch. I find the back door in the kitchen.

Keiran has brushed the snow off a patio set and is waiting for me in the silver twilight. I sit the socially appropriate distance from him.

"Oh!" I say. "I left my phone inside."

"You don't need it to enjoy this Christmas card scene." Keiran takes off his mask.

He's right. It's so pretty outside. The snow is still falling, but it's not has heavy as this morning. I can see the Atlantic coming towards me. It is a light shade of blue in the growing darkness. There's a sharp smell of pine needles from the holiday wreath adorning the back door.

I hug the blanket closer, enjoying the moment.

"Judy moved out west, to Alberta," Keiran says.

"I saw that. She seems busy, as a doctor."

"Not so much since she had kids. She takes holidays now. You two used to be similar—very driven."

"I wonder if we still share the same taste in movies." I snuggle into my chair. "My all-time favourite is the one we watched with you."

"I remember it." Keiran hollers and slaps his leg. "The black and white comedy with the werewolf who became a vegetarian. It's my favourite, too."

As Keiran and I talk about our younger years, my headache fades.

There's something about this man I'm enjoying. He's funny and tells a good story. It doesn't hurt that he's handsome.

I'm having a good time reminiscing and laughing. Then Keiran's phone rings, bringing me back to the present.

"Sorry," he says. "I've got to get this. Have a good night." He jumps down from the porch while answering his phone. "Hi, honey."

Oh.

My high spirits crash to earth and my headache returns.

Whatever. I don't have time for him, anyway. Besides, I'm only here for Christmas. I'll be back in France before New Year's Eve.

I sigh as I climb out of my cozy nest. Keiran and I had talked for over an hour. It's fully dark out, but I can hear the ocean. The shush of the waves is soothing but I have things that must be done. It's going to be a late night.

●

I yawn as I prepare my breakfast of coffee—with milk—and instant oatmeal. I have piles of emails and texts, which have built up while I slept. In the

wood-panelled den off the kitchen, I eat and work at the same time.

Thoughts of Keiran interrupt me. We'd had such a nice conversation last night.

I wonder who his girlfriend is. I log into Facebook to lurk on his profile. There are photos of him and Judy's children in a sailboat, as well as a picture of Keiran with an attractive woman beside him, outside his family's grocery store. The woman has long, straight red hair and a crop top showing off a taut stomach. She's near his age, if not younger.

That must be the honey. I click away from the photo.

Oops! I've accidently added Keiran as a friend. My whole body heats up with embarrassment. How high-schoolish.

This is why I should have stayed in Europe and worked over Christmas. Immersing myself in my professional life means I don't have to deal with my personal life.

I do have friends in Paris. I'm not a hermit. But I've never wanted the husband-and-kids package. I don't know how I'd fit them into my day.

I bury my head in estimates again. Numbers are good at chasing away feelings.

My phone rings. It's my Mom calling to check in. I know my parents worry about me being alone in France, and here. But really, I'm fine.

I take a swift look at the view outside my window. The rain never arrived and the sun is shining in a brilliant blue sky that matches the ocean. The snow tones down the warmth of the scene. It's cold out there. The fire crackling in the grate behind me reminds me to get back to my job.

A Facebook notification pings.

Keiran has approved my friendship. It makes me smile, then grimace.

He's sent a message, too.

Hi Tamzin. Thanks for wanting to be my friend. ;) I wanted to reach out to you but didn't want to be unprofessional and use your contact info from the store. How about sharing a glass of wine with me this evening? Back porch around 9? I'll bring the wine and my own glass.

"Urgh," I groan out loud. I put a hand to my forehead. I'm already behind.

Nine p.m. is one a.m., Paris time.

I'm sure I can catch up if I work faster.

OK, I tell Keiran.

At eight-thirty that night, I find myself putting on make-up and selecting a pretty apricot-coloured cashmere sweater. I put on my coat and boots and take the blanket to wrap-up in while I'm waiting for Keiran.

When I hear the purr of his van, I become jittery.

What if we have nothing to talk about? What if he's just being nice to me because I'm his sister's old friend—emphasis on old.

As Keiran rounds the corner of the porch, my heart beats a little faster. He's holding a bottle of wine, two glasses and a bundle of clothing.

"Here." He passes me a blue, down-filled parka, then a pair of sturdy black winter boots. "It's my old coat and my Umma's boots. They ain't pretty but they're warm."

Wow. Keiran has been thinking about me.

I put on the parka. Three of me could fit in it. Keiran's scent wafts up to me. I smell freshly cut summer grass, with a hint of orange.

"Thanks," I say. "The boots look a bit big but they'll be better than these suede things."

Keiran opens the bottle of rosé. He fills my wine glass, then his and sits. His brown eyes sparkle in the December air. The way he leans toward me gives me goosebumps.

I take a sip of the wine.

"How is it?" asks Keiran.

"It's nice."

"It's French."

"I read the label," I say.

"I'm an idiot!" Keiran plants his forehead into his palm. "I should have asked the woman who lives in France what kind of French rosé to bring tonight."

"Really, it's OK." I take a big gulp to prove I like it. "I do know my wines but I'm not a snob. One day, I'd like to open a *bar à vins* somewhere. Maybe in Harbour Blue."

Keiran nods. "I was thinking of doing that in the store. There's a room in the back I could transform into a cozy, intimate spot. Our town needs something elevated, somewhere nice to relax besides the sports pub on Main Street, where the TV is always on at full volume."

"My thoughts exactly."

"So, you'd move back here one day?"

"One day," I say. "I'm only in France because that's where I got my first job. I've built a solid resume and career in Europe. When I'm ready to call it quits, I'll come home."

"That makes me happy to hear. I had to come back. I quit my job as a biology teacher to run the store after Dad died."

"Didn't want to sell the shop?"

"Couldn't do that to Dad." Keiran takes a drink of his wine. "He put his heart and soul into the store. His father handed the business down to him and he felt like it was his duty to keep it in the family. Although he never put any pressure on me or Judy to take it over." Keiran shifts in his chair. "Harbour Blue is not very big. Less than three thousand people, so you get to know your customers. I like the community aspect of the shop, talking to people, keeping an eye on their health, being involved in their lives. It might pale compared to your fast-paced city life but it keeps me busy. Although it's not something I thought I'd be doing at thirty-nine." He gives me a wide grin.

He looks so handsome…and so young.

I automatically put a hand up to my chin, to smooth out the crinkles in my neck. What if he thinks I'm some sort of cougar?

"It must be late," I say abruptly, standing up and letting the blanket drop to the porch floor. "I've got lots to do tomorrow."

Keiran frowns, then stands, too. He holds his wine glass awkwardly in front of him. "Tamzin?"

"Yes?"

"Ah, never mind. Have a good night."

"You, too."

He disappears into the darkness, moving around the side of the house.

I go into the bright kitchen.

It was an absolutely lovely evening but I have to watch myself. I'm beginning to like this man.

Keiran is kind, caring and hot, and not at all age-appropriate. Plus, there's a "honey" in the picture.

Maybe he's taking pity on me. I'm like an elderly aunt he feels the need to look after.

Oh, well. Bedtime for me.

I fall asleep and dream about hulking steel tractors moving down a highway. Every bit of my life revolves around my job. I never get a moment away from it.

•

As per usual, I work all day. Throughout the hours of staring at my computer screen and online conference calls, I peek at Keiran's profile photo.

"Stop it!" I warn myself.

I wish he'd drop by. Hey! I could order more groceries.

I quickly decide I need coffee beans. I order them from Cho's store and wait for the cute delivery man.

When my doorbell rings, I run to open the door with a large smile for…a teenage girl.

"Keiran's not doing deliveries today?" I ask her.

"It's Saturday," the girl says, off-loading the bags onto the step. "He doesn't work on weekends."

Of course. He's probably got lots of other things going on. He has a life. Perhaps he's taking Honey to a Christmas party.

If I had been in Paris today, I might have gone out for a festive cocktail with a friend. It would be a quick one. I always have deadlines pushing me and negotiations to conquer. My to-do list never goes down and my managing director has added to it in the last hour.

I'll need a strong coffee to douse the flames of panic flaring in my chest.

•

Sunday is like Saturday, although it's not like I have time to realize it.

Mid-afternoon and mired in figures, I hear the doorbell ring.

Keiran!

No, it's my sweet parents dropping by.

"We bought you some treats," Dad says, handing me a large tin with Rudolph's picture on it. "Your favourite Christmas cookies."

"Shortbread!" I say. "Thanks. I'll enjoy one at my desk."

"Oh, dear," Mom says. "Can't you take breaks?"

"That's what I'm doing now!"

"Okay." She nods. "We'll leave you to it. Love you."

"Love you, too," I call out after them.

I shut the door, whip the lid off the tin and dig into the cookies. The blonde shortbread melts in my mouth.

I'm biting into my second treat when there's a knock at the door.

Mom and Dad must have forgotten something.

I swing the door open wide.

It's Keiran.

The sight of him in his navy peacoat and tight jeans takes my breath away.

"*Hib.*" I cough, my mouth full of cookies.

"Hi! You have crumbs all over your face." Keiran laughs, gesturing at me.

I brush the shortbread off my chin. I know I'm blushing and it's not because I'm embarrassed.

"Got any tea to go with those?" asks Keiran.

"Coffee?"

"Sounds good. I've got my mug in the van. I'll meet you out back."

I close the door and do a little jump in the air with the cookies in my hands. *He's here!*

While I brew coffee, I put on Keiran's coat and his mother's boots. I get a tray together with the coffee essentials and the cookies. I head outside into the fresh ocean air.

"What a view," Keiran says, pointing to the lively Atlantic. "If I lived in this house, I'd never get any work done."

"I hardly ever remember to look outside."

"What?" Keiran shakes his head. He plunks down into a chair. "What is so fantastic about your job that you can't take a couple of minutes to enjoy the scenery?"

"When I'm retired, that's when I'll enjoy the view." I sit down. "From my wine bar."

"We all need money to live," Keiran says, "but it shouldn't be everything."

"I'm wired this way." I pour steaming coffee into the mugs. "It makes me proud when I know I've done a good job on a tough proposal."

"Take it from me," Keiran says. "You think you have tons of time but you might not. My Dad thought he had years and years ahead of him." He stares at the ocean.

The waves hit the rocks, sending spray high into the air. A seagull hovers over the beach, suspended in time, before soaring off into the horizon.

"My Dad was a great father and I never wanted for anything—clothes, food, attention," Keiran says. "But as I grew up, I realized his whole life revolved around the business. He rarely took vacations and was always in the store stocking shelves and helping customers. Dad had a proverb he always spouted to me and Judy. He'd say, 'You must sleep before you can dream.' A couple of months before Dad died, I asked him what that really meant to him. He told me he was reminding us that things don't just happen. You have to work for them. He said he was going to retire next year, at seventy-three, and take my mother to Australia, somewhere she's always wanted to go." Keiran's chin drops to his chest. "Now it's too late," he whispers, lost in thought.

I let silence fall over us. I sit back in my chair and wait for him to come back to me.

"Dad's death taught me to enjoy life at every moment," Keiran says, turning my way. We shouldn't be waiting for the right time."

"I can't escape my nature. I'm constantly driven to succeed."

"There's a difference between being driven and being a workaholic." Keiran sips from his mug.

"I guess I haven't learned the difference."

"I'll teach you," Keiran says. "I'll stop by every day at two-thirty. I'll sit out here and enjoy this beautiful nature. You can choose to join me or not. It's up to you."

"Is this a challenge?"

"I guess so. It's also how good habits are formed. Do something every day and eventually, it becomes routine."

"You're on," I say. "Now, have a cookie."

"You left me some?" Keiran chuckles.

I laugh too. We spend twenty minutes talking and joking. With every word he says, I find myself falling deeper and deeper for him. I tell myself that I'm simply developing a solid friendship. That's it. That's all it can be.

●

True to his word, Keiran stops by at two-thirty the next day, and the next day, and the next.

The coffee break is good for me. When I return to work, I find nothing has blown up and the world is still going round. I'm not as tense or stressed and I'm sleeping better. Maybe this not working so hard stuff is a good thing.

Talking to Keiran helps me relax. We have things in common, like our distaste for cooked carrots and a love for bad mystery novels. We trade ideas for "our" wine bar and we agree we want to feature local wine. We are aligned on many levels.

Each time he waves goodbye to me, I curb the urge to yell after him and ask him to stay longer.

I can't figure out why he's wasting his time with me. Why is he investing energy in little old me? What is he expecting?

Halfway through my isolation, on December 17th, Keiran brings over an outdoor speaker and plays Christmas carols for us. He croons *Silent Night* off-key from his chair on the porch. He stops singing and leans toward me. "I'd dance with you if it wasn't against health regulations."

"Only seven more days and you can!" I turn beet red. "I mean, you don't have to. You don't have to see me after I get out."

Keiran's brow furrows. "Huh?"

"I figured you're visiting me because you feel sorry for the spinster who works all the time and is all alone during the holidays and needs someone to make sure she hasn't fallen down the stairs."

"Tamzin, that's not why I'm here."

"It's okay," I continue. "You don't have to explain anything to me."

Keiran's phone buzzes. He picks it up.

"Great timing." He stomps his foot. "I've got to go." He strides off the porch.

I hear him say, "Hi, Honey."

The red-haired woman, his girlfriend, must be looking for him. For the first time in a very long while, I feel alone. I'm an independent woman who makes her own cash and is not afraid of silence. I do not need a man to complete me, nor do I believe in that malarky. However, I can't ignore the hole that has just been torn in my heart.

I turn off the festive songs and listen to the ocean instead. Above the crashing waves, seagulls call to each other. Their cries are mournful and no matter how hard I try to keep the tears at bay, I find myself sobbing into the cuff of the parka.

Keiran's parka.

I yank off the puffy coat and throw it inside. My sadness turns to rage. I stomp on the jacket and then kick off the boots and leave them in a pile by the door.

I'll wear my own clothing, thank you very much.

I sink to the floor.

This is all my own fault. I should have stuck with what I know best—work. I will not let myself be swayed from my schedule again. I will not be someone's pet project.

Now where was I?

Right. At my desk.

●

After burning the midnight oil, the next day dawns too early for me.

"Nothing that some coffee can't fix," I say to myself, resisting resetting my alarm for an hour later.

As usual, caffeine does the trick. I'm a maniac today, negotiating a great deal on delivering an oil rig from Alberta to a major energy company in Europe. My managing director sends another big equipment problem for me to solve by the end of the week. Getting a ten-ton, all-terrain crane from Newfoundland to Argentina. Our business never slows down, not even during Christmas, and I'm vital to its success.

My parents drop by with some groceries and I take a couple of minutes to say hello. I scarf down the lunch they made me without tasting any of the delicious homemade pasta and spicy tomato sauce.

I'm on a call when I hear something at the back of the house. Glancing at the clock, I see it's two-thirty.

Keiran must be outside. Waiting for me.

"Stay," says my head.

"Go," says my heart.

My head wins. Kind of.

Hmmm. If I lean to the right, I can see out of the den to the kitchen window and spot a slice of the back porch, and maybe Keiran. I'm at a ninety-degree angle and my chair is almost at the tipping point.

Damn that man!

Despite being annoyed at my feelings for him, I can't help but want to rush outside to see him. If this call wraps up in a few minutes, I'll go.

An hour later, I'm still trying to get a crane from Point A to Point B. My brain is humming with stress and my neck is as rigid as a candy cane. I massage one shoulder at a time to ease the tension.

My muscles are still taut when I go to bed several hours later.

●

I can't sleep. I keep having nightmares about tractors falling off bridges. Honey, Keiran's red-haired girlfriend, tells me it's all my fault.

I wake up sweaty, cold and wired. It's no use trying to go back to bed so I dress and head down to the den.

It's three a.m. when I sit in front of my laptop to work.

Around noon, my stomach growls. I leave my spreadsheet to heat some canned soup and make coffee. I bring my meal back to the den and put it beside my computer. I'm chilly so I take a minute to build a roaring fire in the fireplace.

The heat from the flames makes me drowsy. "I'll sit on the sofa and shut my eyes for a couple of seconds," I tell myself as I drift off. "Just a couple of seconds…"

I wake up to darkness. I look at my phone. It's just after five p.m. I have missed many calls, texts and emails.

I groan. I also missed Keiran's visit, and not on purpose this time.

I walk into the kitchen and bend to pick up his coat by the back door, still sitting where I had left it the other night. I notice something pale gleaming on the porch in the December moonlight.

I turn on the light and see an envelope propped up against a bottle of rosé, on the patio table.

I hurry out and grab them. Back at my desk, I open the card.

Tamzin, I was hoping to see you. You must be incredibly busy. Fingers crossed it's not because you find me too charming. Here's an early Christmas present. I found this rosé the other day. It's from a local vintner in the Gaspereau Valley. Let me know your opinion. If you like it, I'll put it on the list for our wine bar.

From, Keiran

"*From*?" I say aloud. You put "from" on notes to your dentist. That "from" puts it all into perspective. He's being friendly despite me being a cantankerous old lady.

Might as well open this bottle and gave him my opinion on it tomorrow.

It's actually a great wine. Floral on the nose, with hints of strawberries. It's dry and a bit fuller-bodied than I expected. It goes well with my microwavable chicken dish. I could finish the whole bottle but I know if I do, I'll be toast tonight.

Instead, I finish some estimates before going to bed.

The rosé does put me to sleep and I don't wake up feeling groggy or tired in the morning. I throw open the white linen curtains to a grey sky and rain. Freezing rain.

Ice is forming on the thin bare branches of the poplar trees skirting the shoreline. The trees bow under the weight.

My heart slumps, too. The roads are going to be too slippery to drive. I don't think I'll be seeing Keiran today.

At my laptop, I send him a message thanking him for the wine and telling him I loved it. I add, *Thanks for being a friend. See you tomorrow.*

I can't help but check my inbox every couple of minutes for the first hour of work.

Eventually, my focus turns back to my tasks at hand. This is what I know. This has been my life for a long time. Just because a person is nice to me at Christmas, doesn't mean I should change everything.

Towards midnight, my phone pings. It's a text from Keiran.

Just saw your message. It's been crazy at the store. A pipe burst and there's water everywhere. Will check in with you tomorrow.

He is being a good friend.

●

It's December 21st, day eleven of my quarantine. Christmas Day is less than a week away. I wouldn't have known that if it wasn't for the baking my parents drop off. They tell me the house is decorated and they have put the gifts my assistant Andre sent them under the tree. Mom and Dad can't wait for me to come home.

I'm grateful for their happiness, not to mention the apple pie I have sitting on the kitchen counter. It brings some festive cheer to a long morning.

Around one p.m., my phone rings.

"It's Keiran." His voice melts my heart. "It's the winter solstice today. Usually I'd go to the beach for a stroll but I've got to stay at the store and wait for the plumber. Tell me, how does the ocean look today?"

"I'll check." I walk out onto the porch. "Oh! The water is spectacular. It's a deep blue, almost tropical, and seagulls are bobbing on the waves."

"That makes me smile. Thank you."

He makes me smile. "You're welcome," I say softly.

"Sometimes, it's the little things that matter. Chat tomorrow?"

"Yep. Bye."

I hang up and sit down. I don't have my coat and the cold air encircles me in an icy embrace. I stay and feel the chill. I want to feel something other than the pressure of deadlines and stress tightening about my head, and the deep tiredness that my body tries to hide with coffee and more coffee.

I have money, beautiful things, and I can go anywhere in the world. Nevertheless, where is my joy? Christmas is a magical season, full of family and friends getting together, laughing together, eating together.

When I was young, I loved watching my parents open the gifts I had wrapped with care. I don't even know what I got them this year. Andre ordered everything and signed the tags for me.

What is my reason for working long hours and never taking a vacation? No one in my office has ever said thanks. No one has ever told me to put myself first, to take a rest. I've been pushing myself so hard all these years and it's finally catching up to me. I can't keep lying to myself.

So you know what? I'm giving myself a break.

Keiran may be young but he's wise. He has taught me more in almost two weeks than anyone else. My heart might always skip a beat when I see him but I can settle for the next best thing, being his friend. I'm lucky to have him in my life.

Back in the house, I shut down my computer. Shut off my phone. Turn on the stereo and sing my heart out to *Jingle Bells* while dancing around the living room. It feels great to let loose. To not be watching the clock. It's my Christmas gift to me.

●

I start the next morning in discussions with my managing director. I ask for the next several weeks off and he begrudgingly gives them to me.

"No one deserves it more than you," he admits.

"I know!" I say, before ending the meeting with a click of my mouse.

I drink a glorious cup of coffee, slowly, on the porch. Then I lie in a hot bath with a good mystery book, until the pages are too soggy to turn. I take my time getting dressed before heading to the kitchen.

My heart races when I think about the man who will be here at two -thirty. I'm excited to see him but I can control my emotions.

I put together a tray of festive goodies and make some tea, in time to see Keiran settling into his chair on the porch.

I wrap myself in his coat and bring the food outside.

"What's all this?" He eyes the mound of treats.

"It's a thank you."

"For what?"

"For showing me that a career should not be my life. For showing me how to take a break. You've been a good friend these past couple of weeks."

"You're welcome." Keiran stares at his hands. "But I don't want to be your friend."

I freeze as I'm about to pour him some black tea. My heart and soul twist and turn and wretch themselves out of my body. They drop to the snowy ground and shrivel in the frost. I'm a fool. Of course, he wants nothing to do with me.

"Do I get any tea?" chuckles Keiran, "or are you serving salt air?"

I force myself to smile and tip the teapot towards his cup.

I can't concentrate. Everything around me blurs.

I want him to leave. *Now.* Then I'll go back to work and forget he exists.

"What's wrong?" Keiran asks.

I put the teapot down with a clang. "What's wrong?" I say through gritted teeth. "I'm embarrassed. You just said you don't want to see me anymore. I get that you have a girlfriend but I thought you and I could at least be friends."

"Girlfriend?" Keiran wrinkles his nose at me. "I don't have a girlfriend."

"Yes, you do" I sit up as straight as I can in his oversized parka. "She's called you a couple of times while you've been here."

"I don't have a girlfriend, so no girlfriend could have phoned me."

"You called her honey."

Keiran shakes his head. He laughs and laughs. He laughs so hard, he doubles over.

"It's not funny."

"Honey. *Honey...*" gasps Keiran, "is my employee's name. She answers phones, gets orders ready and runs the store while I'm on deliveries."

"Who is the woman with you on your Facebook page then?"

"That's her. If you look closely, you'll see we're in front of the store. It was a promotional shot." Keiran has tears in his eyes from giggling so much. "You're right, though. She has called while I've been with you. Both times she had a customer at the till and needed my help. I didn't explain that to you because I didn't want to waste your time."

"Then why don't you want to be friends with me?"

"Because I'd like to be more."

Oh.

"I've had a crush on you since I was a kid," Keiran says. "I was going to tell you that first evening on the porch but I didn't want to weird you out."

"It might have," I admit.

"You were like an angry zombie the first day I delivered your groceries. I remembered how vibrant you used to be and I could see hints of the person I used to know underneath your frown. I wanted—*want*—you to be happy."

"I thought you were simply checking on your sister's old lady friend," I say. "Seeing you made—*makes*—me happy."

We sit in silence for a moment, listening to the gulls talk to the waves.

"Pretend I'm holding your hand," Keiran says. "I know you have to go home to France, but I'm wondering if you'll spend some time with me when you're out of isolation."

I glance shyly at Keiran. "How about dinner with me and my parents on December 23rd?" I ask. "Be there at noon."

●

I blast Christmas tunes as I pack my belongings into a couple of suitcases. I have to laugh at my new Parisian boots, which didn't make it one second in Harbour Blue. It's the day before Christmas Eve and my parents are coming this morning to drive me home.

Keiran makes me feel something I've never felt before. My feet don't touch the ground and my head is in the clouds and my heart is full of sugar and spice and all things nice.

I don't notice my phone beeping when new emails arrive in my inbox.

"Do you need to check in with work?" asks Dad while loading the car with my stuff.

"Nope," I say. "I'm on vacation."

"I can't wait to ask Keiran how he made you take a holiday," Mom says. "Let's go home."

True to my parents' words, the house is decorated from top to bottom in Christmas fare. Wreaths, bows and twinkling lights cover every surface. I start unpacking when a vehicle outside honks and honks again.

My heart soars and I run to the front door, flinging it open.

"How rude!" I shout to the handsome man climbing out of his green van.

Keiran's eyes widen. "I'm so sorry."

"I'm kidding." I laugh as Keiran strolls up the verandah steps, stopping a couple of metres away from me.

"Hi," he says.

I stare at the man standing in front of me. I'm afraid to blink in case he disappears. I can't go another second without him. "I have something for you." I reach into my pocket and pull out a piece of paper. "Merry

Christmas."

"What's this?" Keiran asks.

"It's an estimate for moving my things from France to Nova Scotia. And a budget for our wine bar."

"You're staying in Harbour Blue?"

"I'm not good at this feelings stuff," I say. "But I feel like I'm home when I'm with you."

Keiran smiles and points to something green and leafy hanging from the verandah ceiling. "Mistletoe," he says. "Get over here so I can kiss you."

"Go," says my head.

"Go," says my heart.

Lea Storry (yes, that's her real last name) is a writer who owns a memoir writing, editing and publishing business. She can also fly a plane and throw a Frisbee, but not at the same time. Lea lives with her husband in Edmonton, Alberta, Canada.

Visit Lea's site: https://ourfamilylines.ca/

Because of the Christmas Stroll

Debbie Mumford

Jane Ann Kremetz experienced an interesting mix of exhaustion and exhilaration as she hurried along the snow-packed street. The Christmas Stroll always had that effect on her. In the weeks leading up to the annual holiday event, she worked until she could barely stand. She was responsible for making sure everything ran smoothly, ensuring the community a memorable experience. When the big day arrived, she received a jolt of energy from Main Street's festive atmosphere and the strollers' delighted chatter. That buzz always lasted until she fell into bed long after The Strolls' lights dimmed and the revelers returned home.

This year, like every other year, Main Street was closed to traffic for the free community event. Folks would turn out in droves to stroll the six-block stretch, singing carols, munching cookies and candy canes, and buying last minute Christmas gifts. There would even be horse-drawn sleigh rides available for those who tired of walking. Bright lights, festive decorations and snow.

Lots of snow. Jane Ann grinned. If there was one thing Bozeman, Montana could be counted on for, it was snow!

Pedestrian traffic was still light, but that would change soon. Jane Ann had just finished supervising the gingerbread house decorating contest at the community center. Now a group of stalwart volunteers were moving the finished masterpieces to the Main Street bank lobby where strollers could marvel at the local children's ingenuity. Jane Ann was off duty for the rest of the evening. The Stroll would officially begin in a few minutes, and she intended to enjoy the event to the fullest.

Dressed in her warmest down jacket and ski pants, her fingers protected by thick woolen mittens knitted in a snowflake pattern, Jane Ann pulled her jacket's fur-trimmed hood over her head, covering the matching knit cap. Her warm breath puffed out, creating a tiny white cloud as it hit the late afternoon air. She patted her pocket, reassuring herself that her neck gaiter hadn't fallen out. She'd need it before the night was over—December in Montana was frigid.

Following her afternoon of kids and gingerbread, she craved a cup of steaming hot cider, and she knew just where to find it. She hurried past storefronts decorated in their holiday best—twinkling lights, plastic snowmen and reindeer, model trains circling ceramic villages, and of course Christmas trees, whether artificial or the real thing. She aimed for her best friend's bookstore, *A Novel Experience*. Charity always had hot spiced cider and fresh baked snickerdoodle cookies available during The Stroll.

Jane Ann had almost reached the warmth and light of *A Novel Experience* when someone bumped into her, almost knocking her to the ground. A pair of strong hands in leather work gloves steadied her. She glanced up into the concerned face of a man.

A man she knew.

A man she hadn't seen since high school and had frankly never expected to see again.

"I'm so sorry." He released her as soon as she was on her feet. "I wasn't watching…" He peered into her face. "Janey? Is that you? I don't believe it."

"Hi, Chuck," she said. "What brings you back to Bozeman?"

●

The Christmas Stroll was in full swing, the street filling with happy crowds. Excited children dashed from display to display, while their parents alternately called out cautions and chatted with friends. Shops were packed so tightly, customers could hardly move, but no one minded. Christmas spirit ruled, plus there were free brownies, cookies and cider for all.

The event was a huge success, but Jane Ann hardly noticed. She was in a daze. A Chuck Henzel-induced daze. After nearly knocking her over, Chuck accompanied her to Charity's bookstore. There, Jane Ann watched fondly as Charity lost her mind.

Chuck and Charity were twins, but the devilishly handsome man evidently hadn't warned his sister he was coming home for Christmas. When Charity managed to stop bouncing and squealing, she composed herself, then swatted Chuck on the shoulder.

"You know I can't leave the shop during The Stroll." Charity gave him an accusatory glare. "You planned it this way."

Chuck laughed, a warm, deep rumble. "Maybe. But you can't expect me to miss The Stroll just because you have to work, can you?"

Charity rolled her eyes, but her expression showed nothing but delight. "I suppose not." She turned to Jane Ann. "Keep an eye on him, will you, Janey? I don't want him disappearing before I get a chance to visit with him properly."

"Hey, now," Chuck protested. "I'm home for the holidays. Janey doesn't need to babysit me." Then he cocked his head and winked at Jane Ann. "Unless you *want* to babysit me, that is."

Jane Ann's cheeks heated, and she knew her fair skin was lighting up like Rudolph's nose. She opened her mouth to respond, but nothing came out. Chuck's sudden appearance after so many years of absence had robbed her of witty banter. Needing something to do, she grabbed a cup of Charity's spiced cider and sipped. The warmth of the liquid soothed her, while the taste of tart apples combined with cinnamon, ginger and cloves helped clear her mind.

She ignored Chuck's teasing comment and turned to Charity. "He's not going anywhere. Not without seeing your folks and Ed and the kids, but…" She slid her gaze sideways, to the man in question. "I'll be happy to stroll with him, if he'd like."

There. She'd lobbed the metaphorical ball straight back at him, where it belonged.

Chuck laughed again. Jane Ann thought she could get used to that distinctly masculine rumble. "Caught in my own net." He waved at his sister and held out a hand to Jane Ann. "Come on, Janey. Let's see what Bozeman has to offer these days."

An hour and a half later, after visiting every square inch of The Stroll and even indulging in a sleigh ride, Chuck and Jane Ann stood in front of the gingerbread house exhibit for the second time.

"Tough choice," he said. "I know you like that Victorian with the frosted trees and the skating pond made out of blue sprinkles, but I'm partial to that little log cabin over there." He pointed to a very simple confection, constructed to look like stacked logs with icicles of white frosting dripping from a roof shingled with light gray wafer candies.

"Well, I may be biased since I supervised the contest and watched all of these houses being built." Jane Ann smiled up at him, still surprised by how tall he'd gotten. He must have had a growth spurt after high school. "You wouldn't believe how hard these kids worked. Their concentration and attention to detail was impressive."

Chuck nodded. "I can see that. These are a lot better than the ones I remember making."

She laughed. "Yes, but you were always more interested in eating frosting than in building a house."

"Guilty as charged." His eyes sparkled. "I don't know about you, but I'm about strolled out. Want to grab a pizza and warm up?"

She glanced at her watch. The Stroll still had an hour to go. As one of the organizers, she should really stay until the end. Then again, no one was expecting her to do anything further. The need to stay was just her over-developed sense of responsibility. Besides, pizza with Chuck sounded great. A perfect end to a perfect Stroll.

"Sure," she said with a nod. "Let's do it."

●

A surprisingly short time later, Jane Ann found herself seated across a table from Chuck at *The Pizza Parlour*, a favorite haunt from their high school days. Divested of her winter outerwear, she felt oddly exposed and vulnerable, as though her down jacket, mittens and cap had been armor, protecting her from…what?

She glanced at Chuck as he studied the menu they'd both memorized back in the day, and frowned. Why in the world would she be feeling shy and ill-at-ease around Chuck, of all people? He was practically her brother. She knew her best friend's twin as well as she knew her own father. At least she had before he left town.

The man sitting across the table from her was undoubtedly Chuck, but at the same time, he wasn't. The last time Jane Ann had seen Chuck, he'd still been a gawky teen, not yet grown into his full height. He'd had a puppy-ish look, his hands and feet too large for his body. But this Chuck… There was nothing gawky or immature about this man. This was a well-built male in his prime.

The man absolutely exuded masculinity, which confused and startled Jane Ann.

Chuck dropped the menu, met her gaze, and grinned. "What do you say? Shall we stick to an old favorite, or be adventurous and try something new?"

She froze, her mouth dry and her heart pounding. He was talking about pizza, she knew he was talking about pizza, but her traitorous hormones hijacked her brain and dragged it in an entirely different direction. Forget the old favorites. Jane Ann wanted nothing more than to have an adventure—an amorous adventure!—with the delicious guy across the table.

Her cheeks flamed. She dropped her gaze to the menu and shrugged. "Whatever," she mumbled. "You choose."

Chuck reached across the table and took her hand. "Janey? Are you okay?"

His use of her pet name broke her hormones' hold on her brain. This wasn't just some good-looking guy she could drool over. This was Chuck! She'd grown up with him. He was Charity's twin, and the closest thing Jane Ann had to a brother. She needed to get a grip.

Forcing herself to calm, she raised her eyes, met his gaze and smiled. "I'm fine," she lied. "Long day. You're the returning prodigal. You choose the pizza."

He grinned and pulled his hand back. "Pepperoni with extra cheese, it is."

While they waited, a bit impatiently, for their pizza, Jane Ann drowned her inexplicable discomfort in conversation. "So, where have you been all these years? What's up with you?"

"You know I joined the Marines right out of high school?" He rubbed his close-shorn hair. The style suited him. "That's kept me busy. Still does, as a matter of fact."

She eyed his red plaid flannel shirt and blue jeans. "You're still a Marine?"

He leaned back in his chair and studied her. "Sure am. Is that a problem?"

Her cheeks burned, again. "Not at all, but you're not in uniform."

"I'm on leave." He shrugged. "Besides, I don't live in my uniform, even on base."

"I can't believe I haven't seen you since high school. How have I managed to miss your visits?"

"Well, let's see now. The first time I came home, you were in Seattle. I think Char said you'd followed a guy you met at university?"

She narrowed her eyes and hissed. "I did *not* follow him! I was just there for a visit."

"Ri-ight," he drawled with a knowing smirk. "The next time you were hiking in Yellowstone. With another guy." His expression grew serious. "The next thing I heard, you were married. To the Yellowstone guy?"

Jane Ann sighed. Charity had obviously kept Chuck well informed. "Jeremy and I married just a few months after Charity married Ed. I was surprised you didn't come home for her wedding."

He shrugged. "Couldn't. My team was deployed."

A little frown creased her brow. "Really? Where?"

Wiggling his eyebrows and twirling a nonexistent mustache, he said, "I could tell you, but then I'd have to…"

She laughed and raised a hand. "I get the picture."

Their pizza arrived. Jane Ann breathed in the delicious aroma of

Italian spices, tomato sauce and crispy pepperoni. She and Chuck pulled slices onto their plates. Conversation ceased while they enjoyed gooey cheese, greasy bread and heavenly sauce.

With the edge removed from her appetite, Jane Ann restarted the conversation. "So what about you? Married with kids like your sister?"

He paused with the remains of his third slice of pizza halfway to his mouth. "Seriously? You think I'd've showed up at the Christmas Stroll alone if I had a wife and kids?" He shook his head. "Just because you're an independent woman whose husband doesn't mind you wandering around without him doesn't mean I'd leave my wife alone while I came home to Bozeman."

Interesting. Chuck was still single. And Charity hadn't kept him up to date on everything.

"Jeremy and I divorced two years ago," Jane Ann said quietly. She popped the last bite of pizza crust into her mouth. Chewing gave her an excuse not to elaborate.

Chuck dropped his pizza, wiped his fingers on a napkin, and reached for her hand. "Janey, I'm sorry. Char didn't tell me."

"No reason she should have." Jane Ann grabbed a slice of pizza she didn't really want, so she could pull her hand from his. The sizzle his touch engendered had startled her so much she'd almost jumped.

Taking a bite of the new slice, she slid her eyes toward his familiar, yet strangely unknown face. She needed to be very careful around the man Chuck had become. He was entirely too sexy. Her body was not reacting as it should to a guy who was practically her brother!

•

The next week was torture for Jane Ann. Everywhere she went, she ran into Chuck. She'd expected to see him at *A Novel Experience* and, of course, he'd show up at Charity and Ed's home, or the twins' parents' ranch. But the grocery store? The library? The Chamber of Commerce where she worked as a community organizer? Come on!

Every time she turned around, she came face to face with Chuck

Henzel. And every time, her body reacted as if she were a dog in heat! It was embarrassing. Definitely embarrassing and possibly even humiliating.

She reacted to Chuck like she hadn't to any man since she'd divorced Jeremy. Truth be told, her visceral reaction to Chuck was a magnitude greater than anything she'd ever felt for her ex-husband. She couldn't wait for Christmas to be over and for Chuck to disappear back to whatever faraway place he normally inhabited.

During their many—too many in her estimation!—encounters, she'd learned that Chuck wasn't just a Marine. If there was such a thing a *just* a Marine. He was the Element Leader of a Tactical Element of Marine Raiders, a special operations team of elite warriors.

She couldn't imagine it. Chuck, the mischievous boy Jane Ann and Charity had spent so much time avoiding during their childhood, was now the Marine equivalent of a Navy SEAL!

And yet, Chuck was still Chuck, and when her hormones weren't running wild, she enjoyed his company immensely.

Finally, Christmas Eve arrived. Jane Ann joined Charity, her husband Ed, and their two little ones at the Henzel ranch, as she had every year since her own parents had retired to Florida.

Lugging her overnight bag from her cherry red Jeep into Charity's parents' spacious home, Jane Ann called her greetings, raced up the stairs to the bedroom she used every year, and threw open the door.

Chuck stood in the middle of the room, wearing nothing but a towel.

She gasped and stared open-mouthed at the stunningly sculpted muscles on display for her ogling. Everything about the man was perfect, from his ridged six-pack to his well-defined pectorals. Even his calves were perfectly formed. He looked like he'd been chiseled out of marble. Warm, inviting marble.

She yanked her gaze from his gorgeous body to his face and closed her mouth before she drooled on the carpet.

His gaze locked on hers. His eyes darkened with a predatory gleam.

She didn't know whether to run from him or throw herself into his arms.

He took a step toward her, then closed his eyes and inhaled deeply. When he opened them again, the dangerous gleam was gone. "Hey, Janey. Guess Mom didn't tell you she'd rearranged the sleeping quarters?"

Jane Ann felt a deep need to tell him she was more than willing to share the queen-sized log-frame bed with him. She stifled the urge. Good thing too, as Charity ran down the hall and stopped behind her.

Charity took in Chuck's state, reached past Jane Ann and pulled the door closed, then grabbed her friend's arm and hurried her down the hall. "You're bunking in the kids' room this year." Her voice was high-pitched and a little strangled. "We've got cots set up for the kids in our room."

Jane Ann swallowed. Saliva had pooled in her mouth. "Sure. No problem. You sure you and Ed don't mind? I could share with Jilly and Jerry." Twins, especially the boy-girl variety, seemed to run in Charity's family.

Charity laughed. "No way would I put you through that. They'll be up at the crack of dawn and bouncing off the roof beams. Santa's coming, you know!"

Jane Ann laughed with her friend. The tension of her encounter with Chuck seeped away, but the memory remained. She figured the image of his near-naked body was scalded into her memory for the rest of her days…and especially her nights.

After dinner, the family gathered around the Christmas tree in the elder Henzel's living room Each family member—and Jane Ann was considered family—was allowed to open one gift. The four-year-old twins, Jerry and Jilly, each chose a present from Uncle Chuck. Jilly received a necklace and bracelet set made of sea shells, and Jerry got a collection of wind-up trucks.

While the kids played with their new toys and the adults watched indulgently, Chuck pulled Jane Ann from her chair by the fireplace. "Come with me," he said quietly.

Jane Ann followed him from the great room, with its beautifully decorated Christmas tree, into the hallway. When they neared the front of the house, he paused in the arched entry to the formal living room. He took her by the shoulders and positioned her under the center of the arch.

Glancing up, she saw a sprig of mistletoe above her head. She returned her gaze to Chuck and raised a quizzical brow.

"I need to check something out." His voice was a deep rumble. Slowly, his eyes never leaving her face, he lowered his mouth to hers.

Jane Ann's heart pounded furiously. He was going to kiss her. Chuck, her almost brother, was going to kiss her. Her mind raced. Should she pull away? Turn her back on him? Put her hand on his chest and give him a push?

She knew that if she touched that marvelously chiseled chest, the last thing she'd do was push him away.

Before she could settle on a course of action, his lips were on hers and her arms were around his neck. She didn't know how they got there. She certainly hadn't intended to kiss him back, but kiss him, she did. With pleasure and thoroughly.

What started as a gentle touch of lips soon deepened. His mouth was so inviting, his lips so much softer than she would've guessed. Not like kissing sculpted marble at all. She not only accepted his kiss, but leaned into it, pressing her lips to his, her mouth opening on a soft sigh of pleasure.

Evidently he took her sigh and her open mouth as an invitation. His tongue immediately invaded.

She tasted him. Coffee and chocolate cake and a simmering spice that was uniquely his own.

Not to be outdone, her own tongue pushed past his, tasting him more deeply.

As their tongues danced, his arms pulled her so close to that marvelously sculpted chest that she could feel the pounding of his heart. She massaged his head beneath his close-shorn hair.

Her heart raced. Her body thrummed with desire. Butterflies

danced in her belly. *This.* This was where she belonged. He was exactly what she'd always dreamed of finding—her perfect man.

Chuck.

Her eyes flew open. Jane Ann wrenched herself from his embrace, panting with the exertion of leaving that hot and heady space. What was she doing? Kissing Chuck? She couldn't kiss Chuck! What would Charity think?

Chuck blinked, then licked his lips with a sexy twitch of that oh-so-talented tongue. "I knew it." He closed the distance between them. "I knew you were the one for me."

She shook her head. "We can't." Her voice was so breathy, even she could barely hear the words.

He herded her into the living room and backed her against the wall. He hemmed her in with a hand on each side of her head. "Why can't we?"

She closed her eyes to block out the intensity of his gaze and took a deep breath. "You're practically my brother."

"I'm no such thing," he growled. "You're Charity's best friend, but you're most definitely not my sister." He leaned in and nipped her lower lip with his teeth. Playfully. Gently. "I've never even considered doing that to Char, but I've been dreaming of doing it to you for years."

She opened her eyes and stared at him, open-mouthed. "For years?" Then she closed her mouth quickly, lest he take advantage and kiss her again. She wasn't sure she could hold out against a second soul-shattering kiss!

"For years," he repeated, his eyes still dark and predatory. "I've dreamed of getting you alone but every time I came home, you were off with some other guy." He closed his eyes and swallowed, "And then Charity wrote that you married the Yellowstone guy. I thought I'd lost you forever, that I'd never have the chance to tell you."

She recognized his pain. She saw him, *truly* saw him, for perhaps the first time. Charity's brother, but not hers. Never her brother. No kin to Jane Ann Kremetz. Just the love she'd been waiting for all her life. "Tell me what?" She wound her arms about his waist and pulled him closer.

"That I love you." He pushed her against the wall and kissed her thoroughly.

When they returned to the great room a few minutes—or maybe it was a few eons—later, Ed had taken the younger twins to bed. Charity looked at them with wide eyes, then squealed and rushed to Jane Ann's side.

Hugging Jane Ann fiercely, she said, "Finally! He's been pining for you since high school."

Jane Ann broke the hug and held Charity at arm's length, noting the tears sparkling on her best friend's cheeks. "Truly? Why didn't you say something? You could've warned me!"

Charity laughed and swatted Jane Ann's arm. "Seriously? Since when do I do his work for him? If he wanted you, he had to figure out a way to win you."

Jane Ann shook her head and laughed. "I'll never understand siblings."

"Sure you will," Chuck said, hugging both of them at the same time. "You've got a sister now."

"Hey, now," David Henzel called from across the room. "What's going on? You planning to let your mother and me in on the secret?"

Ellen Henzel t'sked. "Honestly, Dave! Anyone with eyes can see that Chuck has finally told Janey how he feels." She crossed the great room and took Jane Ann's chin in her fingers. She gazed into her eyes. "And it looks to me like Janey didn't mind a bit!" She laughed and hugged Jane Ann. "Welcome to the family, sweetheart."

David Henzel moved beside Jane Ann as well and patted her shoulder. "Best Christmas present ever!" He winked at his son. "California's going to feel a lot more like home with Janey there, isn't it?"

Jane Ann's knees felt like rubber. Her eyes widened and her heart raced. California? Who said anything about California? She was Montana born and bred. She couldn't move to California! Why, who would plan the Christmas Stroll every year if she wasn't in Bozeman to do it?

Her breathing came fast and shallow. She was hyperventilating!

Desperately, she locked eyes with Chuck.

He'd stepped back to give his family room to welcome her, but now his gaze was calm, but concerned. He cocked a brow at her and opened his arms.

Jane Ann stepped past his parents and into Chuck's embrace. Her panic eased.

Montana wasn't her home. California wouldn't be either, nor would anywhere his military career took them. This was where she belonged, safe in Chuck's strong arms. She could face anything—even California—as long as they were together.

Jane Ann leaned into Chuck's embrace and smiled, remembering how he'd almost knocked her down at the Christmas Stroll. Raising her face to his, she kissed his cheek and then rested her head against his chest. He'd definitely knocked her off her feet this evening. She didn't care if she never found her balance again. She was at home in his arms and that was all the stability she required.

Debbie Mumford specializes in speculative fiction (fantasy, paranormal romance, and science fiction) as well as mystery and historical fiction. Author of the popular *Sorcha's Children* series, Debbie loves the unknown, whether it's the lure of space or earthbound mythology. Her work has been published in multiple volumes of *Fiction River*, as well as in *Heart's Kiss Magazine*, *Amazing Monster Tales*, and many other popular anthologies. She writes about dragon-shifters, time-traveling lovers, and detectives—whether amateur sleuths or professionals—for adults as Debbie Mumford (www.debbiemumford.com). She also writes science fiction and fantasy for tweens and young adults as Deb Logan (www.deblogan.wordpress.com/).

The Invitation

Jasmine Luck

December 23rd, Guys & St Thomas Hospital, London

"Won't be long now. You've already had the x-rays, and you're the sorriest-looking one left," Zara Yung reassured her Aunt, scanning the people remaining in the hospital emergency waiting area.

Aunt Mary glared. "Oh, that makes me feel much better."

Zara beamed, ignoring the sarcasm. "I'm sure a doctor will be along any minute." She took in her Aunt's appearance, a comically large bump on her forehead, big sad eyes—although possibly more for drama than pain—a bruised cheek, and her wrist cradled against her chest. "Can I get you anything? Haribo? Peanuts? A Diet Coke?"

Aunt Mary shook her head impatiently. She started to speak, then stopped, as if a lightbulb switched on over her head. "There is one thing...."

"Name it," Zara said.

"Don't tell anyone else in the family about this?"

Zara chuckled. "Are you kidding? The day I come home for Christmas, my auntie topples off a ladder in the window of her corner store, with half of London pressed up against the glass. The family Whatsapp group is going insane."

She flicked through the pictures on her mobile for her Aunt Mary, and laughed again at the older woman's horrified reactions.

The last picture in the roll was of an obviously fake bunch of mistletoe hanging from the hospital entrance doorway, that she had snapped when they arrived here. It reminded Zara of the discount-store mistletoe her Dad used to buy and hang all over the house, so he would have excuses to kiss her Mum.

How she missed them.

"Mary Cheng?"

Zara looked up. In front of them stood a doctor straight out of a TV show. He was so ridiculously handsome, there was no way he could be a real doctor. His chestnut-brown hair curled over his forehead and at the nape of his neck, as though it had been painstakingly tousled for maximum attractiveness. His strong jaw was peppered with scruff going just a little grey, and his eyes were the warm hazel of her favourite breakfast tea.

He looked drawn. A pair of square, black-framed reading glasses were tucked neatly in the breast pocket of his charcoal grey scrubs. His angular face, warm eyes and scruffy jaw made him the perfect, knock-out combo of refined gentleman and the naughty bad boy mothers warned daughers about.

"Cal!" Aunt Mary exclaimed, perking up. "You were on today? And you didn't bump me up the line? *Aiyah*!"

Zara's gaze flicked between them. "You know my Aunt Mary?"

His mouth curved into a smile, which made him look younger, mischievous and dangerously like someone Zara wanted to spill her secrets to. "Sure do. I'm a regular at your Aunt's store. I'm Dr. Morales." His accent was American. A mix of California surfer with a lick of Texas drawl. The baritone rasp made her shiver with awareness and wonder how other, more intimate words would sound in that voice.

"No chat," Aunt Mary reminded him. Her tone pulled Zara from the daydream. "Focus. I'm hurt, don't you know?"

Cal huffed out an indulgent laugh, and the women followed him through two sets of double doors and into a room of curtained-off beds. The doctor gestured to an empty cubicle. Aunt Mary sat on the edge of the wheeled hospital bed and the doctor drew the curtains around them.

He perched on the edge of the mattress and glanced down at his clipboard. His hands were great, Zara noted. Tanned, wide palms, long and graceful fingers. Hands which belonged to a piano player.

"Why don't you tell me what happened?" he said.

"Tried to hang lights in my shop," Aunt Mary muttered. "Ladder wasn't long enough."

"I arrived at her shop," Zara added. "'I just got home for Christmas. I saw a crowd at the window, a ladder tilted like the Leaning Tower of Pisa, and Aunt Mary rolled up in a curtain. Fairy lights and a bunch of singing toy reindeer were piled on top." Zara paused. "I expect the video's gone viral, by now."

Dr. Morales barked out a surprised laugh, suddenly looking much younger, then rubbed a hand over his scruffy jaw. "I'm sorry. I think that's the first time I've laughed in about twelve hours."

Zara grinned. Could there be a bit of Christmas magic in the air? "Stick around. I'm here all week."

His kind gaze warmed her. Zara had a sudden, fleeting pang. *It's a shame Aunt Mary never invites any Dr. Morales types for dinner.*

"I am in pain!" Although Aunt Mary looked more put out by the lack of attention.

Dr. Morales smiled sympathetically. "Don't sweat it, Mary. I've been a victim of a step ladder with its own mind, before. Can't trust 'em."

"Did you find out about my wrist? Is it broken? Perhaps I should hug you to test it," Aunt Mary said, sounding hopeful.

Zara cringed inwardly. Aunt Mary had always been an incurable flirt.

Dr. Morales' cheeks flushed as he replied, "Good news. The x-ray shows nothing is broken, but try to be very careful with it for the next week or so. I'll prescribe a tubular bandage you can wear over it, which should keep you from making it worse. Don't be afraid to see your GP if the pain changes or gets worse. Ibuprofen, when you need it."

"Ibuprofen!" Aunt Mary exclaimed. "Might as well just stick a plaster on it."

"Ibuprofen will be fine," Cal said, smiling. "You and Adrian might need some help in the store, though.."

"Count me in for that," Zara volunteered. "I usually do a shift or two when I come home. Keep my hand in."

"Zara is my sister's daughter," Aunt Mary added, pride in her voice. "A fast learner. Lightning at maths and English."

Surprise flitted over Cal's face. "*Zara.* You edit that literary magazine Aunt Mary shows me every month."

Feeling her face heat, Zara turned to her Aunt. "You show customers the magazine?"

"Of course! I am proud of all of you. Besides," she added, "I like to brag."

"All right." Clearly amused, Dr. Morales stood and scribbled on his clipboard.

Zara studied his face. She could have cut herself on those cheekbones.

Cal lifted his gaze and she held it for a second, feeling the air between them fill with a million little unsaid things.

"Thanks. And thanks for making me laugh," he said in that gorgeous voice—sugar on broken glass, deep, with the tiniest sexy rasp. "And happy holidays to you both. See you soon, Mary. Good to meet you, Zara."

Zara looked at the ceiling, hoping for a second that some enterprising med student might have hung mistletoe there, as they had at the entrance.

No such luck. Not that it stopped her from imagining how he might lean in. How gentle the press of his lips would be. How he'd take his time over learning how she tasted.

"You, too," Zara murmured, instead.

His gaze lingered on her face, for a moment longer than was strictly necessary, before he turned away and swapped out clipboards. He scribbled notes on the fresh one.

"You better come by the store and help me lift things!" Aunt Mary called to him, breaking Zara's reverie about how Dr. Morales might kiss.

Zara looked away from Dr. Morales—no, *Cal*. Cal was definitely someone she could have romantic fantasies about, definitely a moanable name—with supreme effort. "Come on. Let's get you home," she told

Aunt Mary gently. "I'll call an Uber."

Aunt Mary sniffed. "Do you think I really went viral? Will I be an Internet sensation?" She sent Zara her very best pitiful look.

Zara sighed. "Why not? It's Christmas. Anything could happen."

Aunt Mary looked between Cal and Zara, pursing her lips. "Yes. Anything."

●

December 24th, The Cheng's corner store

The store was busy.

Zara worked the store counter like a pro, her long, swinging dark hair tidied into a low bun at the nape of her neck. After all, she'd grown up here. Raised by her aunt and uncle, she'd spent many post-school afternoons minding the little Seven-Eleven. She'd restocked and tidied before she was old enough to man the cash register.

Mary and Adrian had taken her in, an eight year old with silent, angry eyes, absorbing her frustration and tears, soothing the yawning void inside her after the death of her parents. They'd been on their way back to Zara when their plane crashed over the Pacific Ocean.

Pictures of Zara and her parents decorated the wall behind the register. Whenever Zara came home, she pressed her fingers to her lips and then touched her digits to her parents' faces.

Today, customers flocked through the door, some ladened with festive bags, others dressed up to the nines, ready to party and wanting to neck some drinks on the Underground, get a buzz going before reaching the bar.

This morning, Zara had left her Uncle Adrian fussing over Aunt Mary, upstairs. Zara opened the store and turned up the Christmas tunes. Currently, *Jingle Bell Rock* danced merrily from the speakers hooked up above the cash register.

Her siblings would arrive later today, then it'd be like a party in the place she'd grown up in. It just wasn't Christmas without doing a shift in the store and hanging with the people she loved most.

She served a woman buying a box of low-calorie beer, then assisted a harassed young man who'd forgotten to buy presents for his new girlfriend. Zara pointed him toward the most expensive chocolates they stocked, some raspberry lip balm and a few mini bottles of wine. He left happy, and Zara blew out a relieved breath that some poor girl wouldn't wake tomorrow to deodorant, a family pack of beef crisps and chamomile tea as a Christmas present.

The bell tinkled, tinnily musical, as the front door swung open. Dr. Cal Morales moved to the counter.

Zara swallowed her sound of surprise. "Er…Dr. Morales. Hi."

"Hey." He rubbed a hand over his jaw. It was obviously a habit. Zara wondered how his scruff would feel under her own palm. "I hoped you'd be here."

"You did?"

"Yeah." He reached into the pocket of his smart grey pea coat and took out a napkin. "It's about this."

Zara took the napkin, bemused. She read in her Aunt's handwriting:

Come to Christmas dinner above the store! My beautiful, single niece will be there.

"It was in an envelope left for me at reception." Cal spoke without inflection, but Zara saw his lips twitch.

"I can't believe this! She must have done it while I was in the bathroom! Honestly, Dr. Morales, every Christmas she pulls this matchmaking crap, because I'm the only unmarried kid. Like it's some kind of disease! I'm thirty-three, hardly at death's door!" Exasperated, Zara squeezed her eyes shut, tamping down the urge to go yell at her Aunt.

He made a sound. She opened her eyes to see him biting his lip, clearly trying not to laugh. It shouldn't have been so sexy.

"Are you done?" Zara asked, raising a brow playfully. "This is meant to be my Christmas break, you know."

"Sorry." His shoulders shook and then he cleared his throat. "Sorry. It must be really frustrating."

Zara sighed. "I can't be mad at her. Not when she does things like show my magazine around. Did she also tell you she adopted me?"

Cal nodded.

"So you know what happened to my parents?"

Another nod. "I'm so sorry, Zara."

She drew in a deep breath, and felt...okay. "You know, Dr. Morales, it's *really* nice not to have to go through it with someone new."

"I bet." His gaze had softened. His eyes were so warm and dark. Comforting. "Call me Cal."

They gazed at each other for a second as over the store speakers, Mariah belted out the unofficial anthem of the festive season since forever, *All I Want for Christmas is You*.

"So, um...." Cal broke eye contact, bit his plush lower lip, then added, "I just wanted to come and tell you about the note because, well, I was considering coming to dinner."

"You were?"

They were interrupted by a gaggle of teenagers. Zara served them all cans of diet soda and bags of Christmas-dinner crisps. They left in a cloud of cheap, too-sweet drugstore perfume.

"God, I remember when I was that age...."

Zara grinned cheekily "-And you wore drugstore perfume? Did you prefer cherry or candyfloss?"

Cal laughed, shoulders shaking. "Unscented. I'm sweet enough."

I'd sure like to find out about that, Zara thought.

"About dinner." Cal continued. "I know it seems weird, accepting Mary's invite, but I don't have any family over here, and this year my shifts fall awkward. I'm working Christmas day from seven p.m., then Boxing Day the same. I can't fly home until after. My grand plans consisted of sitting in my flat, watching the Queen's speech and ordering from the awesome Indian takeout across the street. It's not all bad though, I do have Season Eight of *Brooklyn Nine-Nine* to binge on."

"In that case, you've *got* to come," Zara enthused. "My family is loud, annoying and get way too much in everyone's business, but they're family, and that's what Christmas is for."

"Are you sure?" His face lit up.

His smile was contagious. Oh, Zara really wanted to make him smile all the time. "Positive.," she assured him.

"Can I bring anything?"

Zara opened her mouth to speak, when a loud creak made her turn from the counter.

Aunt Mary was balanced precariously on the stairs, her face screwed up in concentration, obviously trying to listen.

"Are you coming to dinner, then?" Aunt Mary screeched across the store at Cal.

"For God's sake," Zara muttered.

"Yes, please." Cal's voice held suppressed laughter.

"Get back upstairs and rest," Zara grated out, thankful the store was all but empty right now.

"It is my store, I can hang out on the stairs if I want!" Aunt Mary shot back, but did as she was told.

Zara listened to Aunt Mary's footsteps retreating. "Are you sure you want to spend the day with my family?" she asked Cal. "It's not too late to back out."

"Who says my family aren't as nuts as yours? Maybe I want a little reminder of the chaos I'm missing out on." He spoke softly, holding her gaze.

"Do they ever try to matchmake you on Christmas?"

He shook his head. "Not yet. But even if they did, I'd still go spend the holidays with them."

"Okay, be crazy." Zara smiled, as her cheeks heated under his attention. "See you tomorrow. Bring something to drink. Or dessert. We always forget sweet stuff."

"Sure. I'm looking forward to it. And to seeing you again." Cal turned, and then stopped, raising an inquisitive brow. "Oh, did you know that a video of your Aunt has gone viral?"

●

"And then she left him a note asking him to dinner and saying I was single. She might as well have set up an OK Cupid profile for me!" Zara exclaimed to her cousins.

She and her cousins were working the store together, a Christmas tradition. It never felt like work when she did it with them. Over the years they'd developed a smooth working routine, peppered with plenty of insults and banter.

Andrew listened with unrestrained glee. He had long been the subject of his mother's matchmaking schemes. He enjoyed the *schadenfreude* now he was immune. He'd always been achingly cool as a kid, and he was no different as an adult. His hair was spiked just-so, his glasses were Ray Bans, and wherever possible he wore Armani or Hugo Boss t-shirts. He worked as a graphic designer and looked the part.

Kristi's dark hair swung to her chin in a gamine cut. Her go-to outfit was a t-shirt and jeans, the former with slogans. Today's read *Jingle Balls,* with Christmas puddings dotting the fabric. She was an art teacher.

The creative streak definitely ran strong in all three of them.

Andrew and Kristi were Zara's cousins, but she never thought of them as less than her brother and sister. They'd defended her at school and taught her life skills. Kristi had always helped with handwriting, while Andrew helped her ride her bike.

"Want me to check OK Cupid?" Andrew asked, now.

Zara threw a Christmas-themed Post-It® at him. "Don't even. I don't want to know."

Kristi wound a strand of her long hair around her index finger, pursing her lips. "But you're okay with Cal coming, right?"

Zara leaned back against the cash register. "Yes. He's away from his family, you know? I wouldn't want to be away from you losers at Christmas. I just wish Aunt Mary would quit with the matchmaking. Every Easter, Lunar New Year, Christmas.... Can't she get a hobby?"

"Er, newsflash, we *are* her hobby." Andrew broke into laughter.

"Go ahead, laugh it up," Zara muttered. "Once she pairs me off, she'll be pressing for babies from you and your spouses. Mark my words."

That certainly shut them up.

Mollified, Zara served another few customers, all of them buying last-minute wrapping paper and Christmas cards (yes, they were all out of Wife ones, no they wouldn't be getting any more in stock until October next year) and lots and lots of sticky tape.

Two hours later, she gratefully flipped the door sign from *Open* to *Closed*, cashed up and locked the door. Kristi restocked the shelves and Andrew hoovered, then mopped the lino floor.

That done, Kristi took a bottle of Prosecco from the fridge in the staff area and popped it open.

The three of them sat behind the cash register with plastic cups, put their socked feet up on the counter and posed for a selfie on Kristi's phone, as they had done every year since Zara had joined their family.

Zara took the first sip of the sparkling wine and sighed. "*Now* it's Christmas."

It might not be a hugely impressive store, but it was theirs. Aunt Mary and Uncle Adrian had saved hard to buy it, and to provide for their children and then Zara.

The Chengs were her family, one she'd choose even if they weren't related by blood. Christmas without them was unthinkable.

She just hoped Cal was ready for utter chaos tomorrow, and a whole load of weird Christmas traditions.

He was an emergency doctor, right? He'd roll with it.

●

December 25th , the Chengs' apartment

The morning dawned bright and cold, splintery light from the gap between the curtains playing over Zara's face as she woke.

It's Christmas!

She might be thirty-three, but Christmas was Christmas and she was with the people she loved most in the world. Plus the handsomest man she'd seen in forever was coming to dinner—

"Merry Christmas!" Kristi yelled from down the hall.

Zara fell back on her pillow and hugged her quilt around her, bubbly with happiness.

Everyone dressed in their new clothes—a Cheng family tradition on Christmas as well as Lunar New Year—and gathered in the living room for breakfast. Aunt Mary hobbled in to remind everyone she was injured, even though her sprained wrist was nowhere near her feet. Someone, probably Kristi, had doodled a Japanese lucky cat on Aunt Mary's tube bandage in red marker.

Mary received the requisite overdone sympathy for her injury, then held court by the Christmas tree, which was festooned with glitter and baubles as well as mini replicas of *ang pao* - traditional Chinese red envelopes given to friends and family and filled with money—and double happiness symbols hand-knitted by Kristi.

Andrew made poached eggs and salmon for everyone, then they settled on the floor in a circle, to sip fizzy wine and open presents. Zara felt warmth permeate every fibre of her being.

She couldn't have asked Cal to not come over. Not when all his family were an ocean away, and she had everyone she loved most within arms' reach. She stuffed another bite of salmon and egg in her mouth. She didn't care that Aunt Mary would try and shove her and Cal together at every opportunity.

For the first time, she welcomed it.

Merry Christmas to me.

•

Andrew had just stuffed the most hideous reindeer-ear headband Zara had ever seen onto her head, when the bell rang.

Kristi clambered over the sofa to beat Zara to the door. She peered into the video camera. "It must be Cal!" she squealed.

"Want to try again? There are some people in Australia who may not have heard you," Zara scolded, but she was smiling as she said it.

"Come in!" Kristi trilled to the intercom. She pressed the door release button.

Andrew, Kristi and Aunt Mary gathered around the door like a flock of paparazzi.

Zara adjusted her reindeer headband and rolled her eyes at Uncle Adrian, who laughed.

"Thank goodness their spouses aren't coming till tomorrow. They're just as bad," Zara whispered.

Uncle Adrian shook his head. "Yep. Andy and Kristi absolutely found their people. That's all Mary wants for you, you know?"

Zara's heart squeezed. "I know."

Her mother, Mary's sister, was no longer here to guide her. Advise her on which boys to steer clear of and which to take home. Hold her when she cried from heartbreak. Cheer her on when she felt that first flutter of love. Mary had been the one to do all that, every day. If some misguided matchmaking was part of that loving package, then Zara could deal with that.

Kristi hovered on the threshold excitedly, holding the door open. As Cal's footsteps grew closer, Zara couldn't help standing on tiptoe to catch a glimpse of him. Her first peek was of an enormous bouquet of flowers which hid Cal's face. The bouquet balanced comically on a clear tupperware box that contained a partially collapsed gingerbread house.

"Hi." Cal's voice came from behind the flowers.

Kristi passed the flowers to Andrew, then took the gingerhead house, and peered through the plastic. "Oh, no! Did I break it?"

Cal laughed. "Nope. It did that all by itself. That's what happens when you combine a guy with no experience in construction with undercooked gingerbread from a ready-mix packet."

Zara smiled at him from across the room. He sent her a wink and her pulse picked up.

He looked good. A dark blue scarf hugged his neck, atop his grey pea coat. His hair had been tossed around by the wind, the brown-sugar curls tousled appealingly. Behind his black-framed glasses, his eyes twinkled with mischief.

If he were her Christmas present, Zara would be very pleased indeed to find him under her tree.

"Come in, come in," Aunt Mary boomed, dragging Cal into the apartment. "Everyone, this is Cal Morales." She introduced everyone at breakneck speed, then added, "Sit down. Have a drink. Can I take your coat? Are you hungry?"

"Um...."

"Let him get in the door," Zara said. She made her way through the excited wall of her siblings to greet him.

Cal bent to kiss her cheek, his stubble tickling pleasantly.

A wave of contentment swept over her. They were so close that if she just turned her head, their lips would meet and she would learn how he tasted. "Hi, Cal."

He squeezed her arm gently. "You look great," he said, very softly.

"So do you. Merry Christmas." She felt her cheeks heat.

"Love the headband. Cutest reindeer ever."

Zara laughed. The antler bells tinkled. "Wait until I've had too much champagne and my nose goes red."

"Less talk, more alcohol," Andrew announced loudly, pushing between them with the enormous bouquet of flowers.

"Can I start eating this gingerbread?" Kristi yelled from the kitchen. "It's delicious, by the way!"

Zara smiled up at Cal. "Welcome to the Christmas madhouse."

He grinned. "It's my family, but with British accents. At this time on Christmas morning, my sisters—who are older than me, by the way—are usually wrestling on the sofa for control of the remote. My Dad sets the kitchen on fire at least once making his awful Christmas Day pancakes. I am well used to chaos."

Uncle Adrian emerged from the kitchen with a glass of fizzy wine and offered it to Cal. "Thanks for coming."

"No, thanks for having me." Cal accepted the wine, let himself be relieved of his coat, and sat on one of the ridiculously oversized sofas—which were one of Zara's favourite things about coming home. Zara sat beside him and inhaled his scent. Crisp outdoors, vanilla and black pepper.

Kristi re-emerged from the kitchen. "Oh good, everyone's here. More presents!"

As usual, Andrew appointed himself in charge of distributing gifts. Zara saw Cal's surprise when two small presents landed in his lap. She'd gone out to get them yesterday. Just a little something, so he wouldn't feel left out.

Aunt Mary opened her gift from Andrew, a framed still of her toppling from the ladder in the shop window. A white graphic showed the number of hits the video currently had. She roared with laughter.

As Kristi started in on gifts from Aunt Mary, Cal leaned toward Zara. "I honestly didn't expect a gift."

"I wouldn't leave you out," she whispered back. "Besides, I knew you were coming. That's more than I could say about some years."

He raised a brow.

"You know how I said my Aunt regularly tries to matchmake me? Well, one memorable year, she had bribed two guys, regular customers at the store, to come. She must have been desperate for Kristi had just got engaged. I had no idea they were coming, but they bought very elaborate gifts. One even wrote a song for me."

Cal half-gasped, and half-laughed. "No."

"Yep. And a ukelele to perform it with. Which hadn't been tuned."

"I'm so sorry," he managed huskily, through a barely contained laugh.

"No, you're not."

"You're right. I'm not. It's too funny. But, I'm glad I'm the one presented for your approval this year. How am I doing so far?"

Zara's pulse leapt. Did he mean he wanted to—

"Cal's turn to open gifts!" Kristi interrupted.

All eyes in the room turned to their guest.

"Thanks, everyone," Cal said, his voice scratching with emotion. "I really didn't expect gifts. Thanks for having me. I hope you enjoy my flimsy gingerbread."

Everyone laughed.

The first gift Cal opened was a reusable mug, shiny glass with a grey silicone lid and heat band.

"For your morning coffee," Aunt Mary piped from her chair.

"Thank you, Mary."

"I am tired of seeing your Starbucks cup. Now I can sell coffee to you. See? We are having a machine installed in the shop next week."

Andrew snorted a laugh.

Cal started to open the next gift, then clocked the label. "From you?" he asked Zara.

"I hope you like it."

He tore the paper and revealed a notebook on which Zara had written with a marker: *Jokes*.

"I wrote all the jokes I could think of in here," she said "So you can laugh more often."

Cal's gaze settled on her for a long moment. Zara looked into his dark brown eyes, bottomless, full of warmth, and felt a little more of that Christmas magic dance through her.

"This was a really kind thing to do," he murmured, his gorgeous voice low and intimate, and she shivered at the delicious tone of it.

"You say that now, but you haven't read any of the jokes yet. They're awful."

"Even better." He held her gaze.

Out of the corner of her eye, Zara saw Aunt Mary give a very obvious thumbs up. She ignored it. It was Christmas, after all.

●

After the third round of champagne, Aunt Mary stood on shaky legs. "I'd better start the dinner."

Uncle Adrian pulled her back down with a telling look. "Zara, your Aunt can't cook with the state her wrist is in."

Zara studied Aunt Mary for a second. Her wrist wasn't the problem. More likely it was her bloodstream, which had been temporarily converted to fizzy wine. "Uh…."

"That's right," Kristi piped up. "Zara, you'd better start the chicken. Mum can't operate the oven like this."

Zara narrowed her eyes at Kristi, who mouthed *sorry!* . She guessed her cousin wanted to avoid baby questions. Kristi got a pass this once.

"Cal can help," Aunt Mary added.

Zara glanced at Cal, who was stifling a laugh, biting his bottom lip.

It was very biteable.

"Sure." He stood, amusement crinkling the edges of his eyes. He was very handsome amid all the Christmas decorations. The string lights picked out the copper-gold in his tousled hair.

When they reached the kitchen, Zara muttered, "I'm, ah, sorry about that." She was acutely aware of him behind her, and the solid warmth of his broad chest.

"Don't sweat it. I imagine if I was home I'd get the same from my Mom."

Zara removed the bagged chicken from the fridge and set out herbs and spices. "Really?"

"Sure. You know, I'm pushing forty-two. Unwed. It's embarrassing for a mother to have to tell her friends that at yoga, apparently. Although being an ER doctor does soothe her pain."

Snorting out a laugh, Zara pointed at the freezer. "Can you get the potatoes out? I'll season the chicken. No one likes turkey in this house."

He did as she bid. Zara watched his hands work. His knuckles were peppered with tiny scars, some old, some new, breaking up the smooth golden tan of his skin.

It was weird, but somehow right, to see him in the apartment she'd grown up in. He fit. He wasn't like any of the other random guys her Aunt Mary had invited back, desperate for Zara to make a connection. Maybe….

"I just realised why she did it," Zara murmured.

Cal set the bag of goose-fat-coated potatoes on the counter. "Hmm?"

"She wanted me to have someone of my own. I'm an only child. After my parents died, I felt so alone. Still do, sometimes, even though I adore the Chengs. They're my family, without a doubt. But she only wanted me to have a love that was just my own. I was so frustrated, I couldn't see that."

Cal held her gaze and smiled slowly, his eyes going warm and soft. "Family can show love in the weirdest ways, huh? But Christmas has a way of clarifying things, don't you think?"

Zara stepped closer. She settled a hand on his shoulder, looked up into his warm brown eyes. She could lose herself in them. "Christmas is also a good time for first kisses. Especially when an enterprising Aunt has hung plastic mistletoe from the kitchen strip light."

"What…?" Cal looked up at the production-line mistletoe, yellowed with age, which hung from the light. He huffed out a soft laugh.. "Who am I to defy mistletoe?"

The sweet mischief in Cal's eyes was pure enchantment. He bent his head to hers, Zara rose up on her toes and they met in the middle. His lips were soft and warm. She sighed into the kiss, breathing him in. It felt magic. He felt like magic.

As they parted, a floorboard creaked.

Zara turned to see Aunt Mary, Andrew and Kristi watching avidly from the sofa. They didn't even pretend to be innocent, now they were caught.

Cal tugged her back to him. "Merry Christmas, Zara."

And he closed the kitchen door.

Jasmine Luck has been published with Jupiter Gardens Press, as well as Rebel Ink Press and Wild Horse Press.

She writes contemporary romance, fantasy romance, and romantic comedy. In 2015 she received a CTRR readers' choice award. Her short story, "Yes, Chef", appears in the *Love All Year Vol 2* anthology, out Sept 2021.

She loves cats (a normal amount, and you can't prove otherwise), reads voraciously, and bakes most days. She lives in the UK with her very patient husband, and one son.

Find Jasmine on Twitter @jazzyluckwrites

The Ghosts of Christmas Present

Karen McCullough

Lyndsey Williams pulled to the side of the driveway and stopped the car, needing a moment to gather her nerve for the ordeal ahead. She switched off the radio, which currently blasted Bing Crosby's *White Christmas,* and stared at the ugly old Victorian house.

A scattering of snow lay on the ground around it, but no decorations festooned the place. None ever had—that she could recall, anyway. She tried to visualize the building with lights lining the porch and wrapping the shrubs along the front, but her imagination couldn't overcome the weight of the past.

Drawing a deep breath, she put the car back in gear, drove up to the side of the house and found a space on the grass at the side, next to a large new pickup truck and an SUV. Farther back, the shabby green Chevy sedan Marnie used to drive sat rusting into oblivion. No sign of Dale's beat-up old Ford pickup. Lyndsay wouldn't be mourning over that.

She'd just gotten out of the car when the front door of the house opened and a group of people surged out onto the front porch. Josh Sanders led the way. For a moment, he was the only one she saw. They weren't blood relatives, but she could never think of him as anything but the most wonderful big brother any girl ever had. He was the sole reason she was there.

He wrapped her in his arms, enveloping her once more in his warmth and strength and whispered, "Thank you for coming."

Lyndsay stared back at him. "You asked." She smiled at the petite brunette beside him. "Jenny, you look..." She stopped for a moment. "Fabulous. Is this what I think it is?" She nodded toward Jenny's midsection.

"Well, I'm not a mind-reader," Josh answered, "but if you're thinking that we're expecting, then you're right."

"Ohmigosh, that's so exciting." She embraced both of them. "You're going to be great parents."

Josh drew a sharp breath. "I don't know. I hope so."

Lyndsey looked behind him and froze for a moment. The middle-aged man was a stranger, but the tall young man with sandy hair was... someone she'd hoped to never see again.

She should've known better. Aaron Hampton had been Josh's best friend for a long time. He'd also been her main crush for years while growing up. The last time she'd seen him was at Josh's wedding, where, fueled by too much champagne, she'd made a complete fool of herself. Even now she felt the heat rising in her face, but she ignored it to greet him with hard-won self-possession.

"Hello, Aaron. It's been a while." She reached out a hand to shake his.

Maturity had only added to Aaron's good looks, refining the lean strength of his features. The wavy light brown hair, blue-green eyes, and dimples in his cheeks hadn't changed, but he'd added some muscle to his rangy frame.

"You're looking good, Lyndsey," he said. "Josh tells me you're now a licensed architect. Congratulations."

"Thanks." She couldn't think of anything more to say.

"I'd like to hear more about it," Aaron added.

Josh saved her the need to reply when he broke in to introduce her to the older man, his father-in-law Tom Farrell, Jenny's only surviving parent. Tom shivered as they shook hands and Josh added, "Let's get Lyn's bags and go inside before we all freeze."

Josh and Aaron each took one of her suitcases, rolled them into the house and carried them up the stairs to her old room. New curtains, bedspread and rug made a brave attempt to cheer up the otherwise bare space.

Once Aaron left them, Lyndsay sank onto the bed and turned to Josh. "You know that I'm thrilled to see you and Jenny again and delighted for you, but what's this really about? Where's Marnie? And why are we making an effort to celebrate Christmas here? She's never been interested in celebrating it before."

He turned the wooden desk chair to face her and sat. "Marnie's in bed. We'll go see her shortly. Lyn...Marnie has cancer. Pancreas. Doc says she has a few weeks more, at most. They wanted to put her in a hospice unit at the hospital, but she refused and insisted on coming home. They'll be sending people to treat her regularly. But I thought..." He stopped and looked around the room. "I wanted to do a real Christmas celebration this year. We're the closest she's ever had to family and this is the only chance she'll ever get."

"She's never wanted one before. Why do it now?" Lyndsay studied Josh's demeanor. "She didn't ask for this, did she? You just decided to go ahead and do it. Why?"

"Because she never really had the chance. Living with Dale..." He looked down at his well-worn Nike sneakers. "It was really Jenny's idea and you know..."

"You'd do anything in the world for Jenny," Lyndsay said. "And I totally approve."

A quick grin flashed on his face and disappeared. "Jenny has taught me so much about happiness and the importance of family. I wanted to share that with Marnie, and we're the only family she has."

"You want to show her what she's been missing all this time?"

"All right. Yes, that's part of it. Not the most worthy part, perhaps."

"Josh, you know I'd do anything in the world for you, but I'm not sure I know how to do this."

"I understand. I'm no expert either. But Jenny is, and her dad is, and they've promised to help us figure it out. Aaron said he'd help, too."

Something twisted in her chest, just hearing Aaron's name. "He's staying here through Christmas?"

"Yup. His folks decided to treat themselves to a cruise to Jamaica and his sister said it was their year to go to the in-laws for the holiday. Do you mind?"

She shrugged. "I don't know. Your wedding…I…this whole thing is kind of mind-boggling."

Josh stood. "I know. It's an experiment. I hope it will work out okay. Let's go see if Marnie's awake."

Lyndsay drew a deep breath. "Okay." Josh probably knew she secretly hoped their foster mother still slept, so she could put off the meeting a bit longer.

"Don't expect that being sick has improved her disposition," Josh warned.

"I don't."

When they got to the hall, Lyndsay turned toward the master bedroom in the back, but Josh nodded the other way. "We moved her to the old den downstairs."

On the way, they passed through the living room and found Aaron standing on a ladder, hanging garland over the fireplace with Tom's help and Jenny's directions.

Aaron glanced their way and smiled, reserving a particularly stunning grin for Lyndsay. Her gut did a peculiar tuck and roll which apparently still happened every time he looked at her.

Her breath caught and her heartbeat sped up. What his lanky frame did for a pair of jeans and a flannel shirt ought to be illegal. She hoped he didn't know the effect he had on her, but after the events at Josh's wedding, he must surely suspect. She nodded in his direction as they passed.

The back den, which had been used mostly by Marnie's husband, Dale, when he was alive, now held a hospital bed with a table beside it.

Marnie had once been a large, robust woman with long, dark hair and a personality that made the unreformed Grinch sound like a sweetheart. The shrunken old woman with the grizzled, tangled hair lying in the bed clashed with Lyndsay's memories…until Marnie opened her near-colorless eyes and glared.

"Didn't expect to ever see you again." Marnie's voice was too cracked and creaky to intimidate Lyndsay the way it used to.

"I didn't really expect to see you again, either."

Josh pushed a chair toward Lyndsay.

Marnie looked at Josh. "You brought her here. You looking for some kind of tearful reunion?"

She meant to antagonize him, but Josh said evenly, "Nope. Didn't expect anything of the sort. Just giving everyone a chance to pay their respects."

Marnie's eyes widened. "Respects? To me?" Her wheezy laugh turned into a cough. She reached for the glass of water on the table beside her and took a sip. "Nobody's got any respects to pay to me. Never needed it. Don't want it."

Lyndsay didn't know what made her say, "Not true. I do have some respect to pay to you. You may not have been happy about it, but you did feed me, clothe me and put a roof over my head. So I owe you for that."

"Sheesh, girl. I did what I had to. They'd have had those welfare people after me for sure if I didn't make sure you were fed and had clothes."

The food had been cheap and often not very plentiful, but Lyndsay hadn't gone hungry often. The clothes had been used, sometimes well used, but usually clean. She'd stayed warm enough most of the time.

One of the social workers had told Lyndsay her birth mother died of a drug overdose in her early twenties, leaving her two-year-old daughter an orphan. If Lyndsay's mother knew who'd fathered her child, she'd never said.

Lyndsay had always understood that Marnie and Dale didn't love them, not the way some of her friends' parents loved their kids. Marnie and Dale had fostered children mostly for the money the state offered for their care. Other foster kids had come and gone, but Lyndsay and Josh stayed. They'd grown close, especially after Dale died.

At fifteen, Josh started working landscaping and construction jobs to earn extra money. He took his position as Lyndsay's big brother seriously and made sure she had everything she needed, particularly for school. He celebrated it as a personal triumph when she graduated high school at the top of her class and was offered several scholarships.

When Lyndsay had left for college, she'd vowed never to return. If she'd had any doubts about the wisdom of that decision, Marnie's behavior at Josh's wedding had confirmed it one hundred percent. The woman was as mean as a snake. Even knowing she was dying hadn't changed her.

"Well, anyway, we're here." Lyndsay made no effort to take the woman's hand or touch her. "Josh says we're going to have a blowout Christmas celebration. I plan to enjoy it. I hope you can too." They were the right words, but Lyndsay wondered if she meant them.

"Waste of time and money," Marnie scoffed. "Useless."

"No, it's not," Josh said. "But you'll have to see for yourself."

Marnie waved a bony hand. "Can't stop you."

"Nope." Josh stood. "We're doing this whether you like it or not."

The old woman closed her eyes. Josh nodded at Lyndsay for them to leave.

One of the hospice workers came in as they went out. Josh took a moment to introduce her to the nurse and update the woman on Marnie's condition.

They followed the sound of laughter back to the living room. Jenny, her father, and Aaron were dressed for the outdoors. The two men carried boxes and were heading for the porch.

"Let's get our coats," Josh suggested to Lyndsay.

"What are we doing?"

"Decorating. Aaron brought a bunch of outdoor lights. Jenny couldn't resist a blow-up Santa."

"Winter Wonderland, here we come," Jenny said.

Over the next hour, they draped strings of light along the top of the porch, the front roofline and gable, and down the sides of the house. Aaron did most of the ladder-climbing to reach the high spots, with Lyndsay assisting by feeding him the hooks and the lines of lights.

Half an hour into the work, Jenny and her dad retreated inside to get dinner ready, leaving Josh, Lyndsay and Aaron to finish the work.

Lyndsay couldn't help watching as Aaron scaled the ladder and stretched to position the hooks. Nor could she resist returning his smiles as they worked together to wind strings of lights around the porch railing. His blue-green eyes still sparked in that devastatingly appealing way. She wondered that he didn't seem to hold what had happened at Josh's wedding against her.

Once the porch was draped, they set up the blow-up Santa out on the lawn in front. The two men shooed Lyndsay inside while they tested everything. They said they didn't want to spoil the surprise when they lit the lights later.

She found it odd they were going to all that effort for a display few people would see, but apparently it was part of the Christmas ritual. Once she'd shed her outdoors gear, she helped set the table for dinner, which was ready shortly after the two men came in, faces reddened from the cold, but cheerfully pleased with their efforts.

The meal was simple—meatloaf with roasted potatoes and green beans—but delicious, and made more so by the company. Jenny and her dad shared stories of Christmases past, some from her childhood and some reaching back to his. They laughed over pratfalls and strange presents under the tree.

After they'd cleaned up, Josh asked everyone to head outside for the lighting of the outdoor decorations. They donned coats, hats and gloves, then Josh asked them to wait a minute.

He disappeared and returned shortly, carrying Marnie, wrapped in blankets.

Lyndsay opened the door for them, and everyone streamed outside, then turned when they were ten feet from the porch.

Aaron went to the side of the porch to plug the lights in.

Lyndsay couldn't hold back a gasp as the front of the house lit up with the small multi-colored lights. The grim shadowy hulk morphed into a fairy castle, warm and inviting, standing out against the night sky and surrounding trees. She'd seen plenty of decorated houses before, but she'd never imagined this dreary place could be so transformed.

She squealed in delight.

Aaron stood right beside her. "It's amazing, isn't it?"

The lump in her throat made the word come out almost as whisper when she answered. "Magical."

"I hoped you'd appreciate it."

She looked at him. The lights washed over his face, accentuating the creases which bracketed his mouth when he smiled and highlighting the glints of green and silver in his eyes. She only got a moment's look though, because he turned to watch Marnie's reaction.

The older woman stirred in Josh's arms and muttered, "I still say it's a waste of electricity."

Lyndsay thought, *same old Marnie*.

Then the woman spoiled her bitter reaction by adding, "It is kind of pretty, though."

Once back inside, Josh took Marnie to her room and settled her for the evening. Jenny made hot chocolate for everyone else and they took their steaming cups to the living room.

When Josh returned, Jenny's dad, Tom, held up a book and said, "When Jenny was younger, one of our Christmas rituals was that on the nights before Christmas, I'd read to the family Dicken's *A Christmas Carol*. Jenny asked if I'd be willing to do it again and I said I'd be delighted. But I have to be sure all of you are interested in listening, too. It's perfectly fine if you'd prefer to do something else, though."

"I've seen a couple of movie versions of it," Lyndsay said, "but I've never read the original."

"No one reads it quite like my dad." Jenny's pride was evident in her tone.

"I've never read it either." Aaron sat at the other side of the loveseat Lyndsay occupied.

Tom settled in an armchair lit by a nearby floor lamp and opened the book. "'Marley was dead, to being with'," he began. He read with a slight English accent and had them all chuckling at the next paragraph, when Dickens questions why a door-nail should be regarded as particularly dead. A few minutes later Lyndsay shivered in alarm with the arrival of Marley's ghost. Tom relayed Scrooge's dialogue in a sneering growl that captured the initial meanness of the character brilliantly.

When he stopped and put a bookmark in the pages right after Fezziwig's party in the middle of Scrooge's adventures with the first ghost, most of his audience sighed.

Lyndsay let out a small protest but Tom just smiled. "We have two more nights before Christmas, and this is about a third of the way through."

They all retired after that, but once Lyndsay put out the light, she had trouble falling asleep. As she rolled around, her thoughts turned to Aaron, and then, inevitably, to Josh's wedding.

She'd just finished her exams at the end of her second year of grad school when she flew back to Massachusetts for the ceremony. It had started so well. She loved Jenny, both for herself and for the way she made Josh so happy. Lyndsay had been thrilled to be a bridesmaid for them, and the service itself, held in the yard of Jenny's home, was beautiful.

The reception was an event from a fairy tale. Lyndsay felt like a princess in the amazing dress Jenny had chosen. Even Marnie had glammed up for her role as Mother of the Groom. The weather was marvelous, the food wonderful and the champagne cold and bubbly.

As Josh's best man, Aaron looked handsome in a tux which showed how his lean frame had filled out. They danced a couple of times with each other, then Lyndsay danced with Josh and two of the groomsmen before Aaron sought her out again. And again.

They matched well on the fast numbers, but when the music switched to a slower ballad, he pulled her against him. Being close to him, moving in rhythm, enveloped in his warm strength, listening to his low voice whisper in her ear how beautiful she looked, made Lynsday wonder if she'd died and gone to heaven. Her blood fizzed with joy. Several glasses of champagne added to the feeling of floating in a magical world.

Champagne had some part in what happened next, too. After several vigorous dances, Aaron led her to the refreshments stand to collect fresh glasses and a few canapes, before they retreated to a secluded corner. They talked and laughed and held hands.

Then he kissed her.

Her heart jumped and her pulse raced. The world faded, lost in the haze of delight that flowed between them.

Lynsday wasn't aware of squirming onto Aaron's lap, or when his hand pushed up her dress to brush her thigh, as they continued to kiss.

A cold, cutting voice, far too close, snapped them out of it. "You slut!" Marnie hissed at Lyndsay. "Just like your mother. I thought I raised you better than this. Blood will tell.."

A group of onlookers had gathered behind Marnie.

Lyndsay jumped to her feet. The blood drained from her face and brain, leaving her swaying before Marnie's tirade. More people approached. Lyndsay thought she might faint. Aaron put a hand on her arm to support her, but she shook it off and ran from the garden, all the way back to her hotel room.

She cried for most of that night, from the humiliation of being discovered and then upbraided in front of Aaron and all her relatives, but maybe even more from the fear that Marnie was right about her bad blood. The next morning she stole out early to get a car to the airport.

She was still so devastated, that she ignored Aaron's calls and messages, and when Josh called from Hawaii, where he and Jenny were spending their honeymoon, she couldn't talk to him about it.

●

Lyndsay woke the next morning to the aroma of coffee filling the house. Once she'd washed and dressed, she followed it as she would a lifeline down to the kitchen. Only Jenny was there.

"You up for a trip to town today?" her almost-sister-in-law asked. "I need to finish Christmas shopping and I'd love some non-male company."

"I need to do some shopping, too," Lyndsay said.

Aaron wandered in and headed straight for the coffee pot. Josh followed behind.

Once they'd finished breakfast and cleaned up, the two women drove into Framingham. Lyndsay had bought a few gifts before she came, but she hadn't known that Aaron or Tom would be there. The two women spent the morning moving through stores and departments, consulting each other on what people wanted or would enjoy. Lyndsey debated about getting something for Marnie. At Jenny's urging she bought Marnie a picture frame. Jenny promised she'd take a photo of Lyndsay and Josh and get it printed right away.

They stopped at an upscale candy and baked goods store, where Jenny bought many boxes of assorted small treats. "Stockings," she said, when Lyndsay asked about it. "Stockings need treats."

They had lunch together at a small café before they made their last purchases, then headed back to the house in the mid-afternoon. On the way home, Lyndsay asked, "Why did you want me to get something for Marnie so badly? You know what she is, what she's like. For that matter, why are we doing this whole thing?"

Jenny drew in a deep breath. "I've heard Josh's stories and seen Marnie in action. But she only has a few more weeks left, maybe only a few days, while you have your futures ahead of you. I don't want Josh, or you either, left with any regrets. It isn't really about her at all. It's about him and you. You can go on knowing you did everything you could to make peace with her." Her voice softened. "You know my mother died in a car accident when I was fourteen. What you don't know is that I had an argument with her, right before she left to go shopping. A real screaming match. If I'd known.... Anyway, every day I wish I could've told her I was sorry, that I didn't really mean all the ugly things I said. Maybe this is my way of atoning for that."

Lyndsay was silent for a few minutes, thinking. "I'm sure your mother knows."

"Maybe. I hope so. But I still have to live with it." She shook her head and shrugged. "Anyway, it's good for my dad, too, to have a

Christmas with more people." Then she changed the subject to her dad's retirement and kept the conversation there until they got home.

●

When they walked into the house, Aaron and Jenny's dad were maneuvering a large fir tree into a stand that didn't look big enough to support it.

Lyndsay and Jenny shed their gear and stowed packages. When Lyndsay returned to the living room, the men were adjusting the tree's position to get it to stay upright. The tree sat in the bay window looking out over the front of the house.

Jenny said, "It's not quite straight, but if we give it a quarter turn you won't be able to tell."

"It smells wonderful," Lyndsay said, as the fresh, piney fragrance engulfed her. "I've never seen a real tree in a house before."

Jenny and Aaron both looked surprised. Aaron said, "Never?"

Lyndsay shrugged sheepishly. "I spent a couple of Christmases with college roommates and their families, but they always had artificial trees."

Aaron shook his head. "Those are okay if you have to have them, but there's nothing like a real tree to make you think of Christmas. You up for helping to decorate it?"

"I guess so. You'll have to tell me what to do."

"It's not hard," Aaron answered. "After we get the lights on, it's mostly just hanging things on the tree."

Jenny nodded to a box nearby. "Help me check the lights." She picked up a string of small bulbs, plugged it in to check that it lit up, then handed it to Aaron. Lyndsay pulled another string out of the box, untangled it and did the same.

Aaron and Tom wound the cords around the tree, working from the bottom to the top.

Josh brought in several plastic containers and a couple of cartons of ornaments.

Aaron dragged the ladder over to the tree to finish the topmost rounds of lights. Lyndsay tried not to be obvious about watching him, while drinking in the way he moved so gracefully up and down the rungs. His relaxed expression and easy smiles said he was enjoying the decorating.

When the lights reached the top of the tree, a debate ensued about whether the star topper should be put in place then, or as the very last thing. Aaron's argument that it would be easier to do right then, rather than when all the hanging ornaments made it more treacherous, seemed logical to Lyndsay, but was trumped by Jenny's insistence that the topper should be the finishing piece. Since both Josh and Jenny's father supported her case, Jenny's wish carried.

Lyndsay remembered Aaron being super-competitive in high school, yet he took his defeat in stride, acceding with a shrug and a laugh. He had matured and mellowed.

He still looked incredibly good to Lyndsay. He had acquired smile lines around the eyes and his sandy blond hair had darkened. He still ran his hands through it when thinking.

Aaron turned to her as he climbed off the ladder, catching her staring.

Lyndsay felt the heat rise in her face, but said, "Can we turn on the lights, yet?"

"Not yet."

"Lots more decorations to put on." Jenny pointed to the boxes.

They festooned the tree with the glass balls, figurines, crystal icicles, bows and ribbons. Aaron handled the higher branches, while the rest of them worked on the lower ones.

Once again, Jenny and her dad disappeared into the kitchen to fix dinner, while Josh excused himself to take a business call. It left just Lyndsay and Aaron to finish the tree.

They worked in silence for a few minutes. Then Aaron dismounted the ladder and waited for her to bring another ornament to him. He moved in front of her and spoke softly. "Lyn, can we talk about it?" His expression was serious, almost grim.

"Talk about what?"

His lips quirked in a brief, wry smile. "The elephant in the room. I never got a chance to apologize for what happened at Josh's wedding. I have no real excuse except that I've wanted you for such a long time. Add in all that champagne, and well…. I know I took advantage of you. And you took the brunt of the humiliation from it. I've felt awful about it ever since. I tried to call to apologize a couple of times, but I can't blame you for not wanting to talk to me."

"You—" She had trouble forming words. She'd never considered that he might feel responsible. "I…. You have nothing to apologize for. It was me. I wasn't myself. I guess the champagne and the excitement made me light-headed."

"That's generous of you, but I have plenty to apologize for. I took advantage of you. You were so sweet. I should've known you were inebriated. Heck, I was, too. In any case, I'm very sorry for what happened. I hope you can find it in you to forgive me."

She was still too startled to know what to say.

He bent and kissed her forehead, then picked up another ornament to put on the tree. "Think about it, will you? It's been weighing on me. Now, let's get the tree finished. Just a few more things to hang."

He'd given her a lot to consider, but moments later Jenny called that dinner was ready and they hurried to add the last couple of decorations to the tree.

Dinner was a cheerful affair and afterward, they held the ceremonial tree lighting, which was similar to last night's outdoor event. Again, Josh carried Marnie in to watch.

Aaron inserted the plug and the tree lit up.

Lyndsay exclaimed in delight. It wasn't the same shock seeing the outdoor lights had given her, but she hadn't anticipated how much warmth it would add to the room, and how very cheerful it was.

Marnie didn't say anything, but she stared at the tree steadily for several minutes, until she sighed and nodded for Josh to take her back.

Lyndsay wondered what emotions moved beneath Marnie's stolid, stoic expression.

Jenny insisted on taking pictures of everyone posed against the tree, in a group, in couples and individually. She took several of Josh and Lyndsay together.

Then the two women sorted through the pictures, choosing the best ones, before Jenny went to the computer to arrange for printing them.

When she was done, Jenny offered hot toddies as an alternative to hot chocolate.

Aaron brought Lyndsay one and sat beside her on the couch—a little closer, tonight. They sipped the warm, fragrant drinks as Tom read the next section of *A Christmas Carol*.

Lyndsay quickly got lost in the magical story of mean old Scrooge and the ghosts of Christmas Past, Present, and Future. She cringed when Scrooge heard himself described by others, especially his nephew's wife. Once again, she sighed when Tom closed the book just as the third ghost was due to appear.

Lyndsay had a lot to mull over as she lay in bed with the lights out, especially her talk with Aaron. She'd never considered the events of Josh's wedding from his point of view. It hadn't occurred to her that he would feel guilty about it. Now she had a new source of chagrin, as she realized that by fleeing from the scene, she'd left Aaron to deal with the embarrassment and the questions from the onlookers.

Really, she owed *him* an apology. She fell asleep on that thought.

●

Christmas Eve began with Jenny announcing she planned to bake cookies that morning. She asked Lyndsay to help her. The guys, Jenny said, could use the time to wrap gifts. She'd left the wrapping supplies in the bedroom she and Josh were using.

Lyndsay admitted she'd never made cookies before and had no idea what to do. Jenny proved to be a patient and cheerful teacher, guiding her through the mixing, stirring, rolling, patting and baking process.

The aroma coming from the oven as the first batch browned provided reward enough for the effort, even before Lynsday sampled them. Biting into a cookie still warm from the oven had her almost swooning. No store-bought version had ever tasted that good.

After lunch, the men settled down to watch a football game while Jenny and Lyndsay wrapped the presents they'd bought.

Once again, Lyndsay relied on Jenny to show her how to do it. "It seems like you're having to teach me everything about celebrating Christmas," Lyndsay commented.

"Not a problem. I had to teach Josh, too. You guys never had anyone to show you."

"True."

Once the gifts were done, Lyndsay looked in on Marnie. A nurse was with her, but she retreated to the kitchen to sample cookies, and to give Lyndsay some privacy.

Marnie's eyes were shut but they snapped open when Lyndsay took her hand. Marnie grimaced.

"Are you in pain?" Lyndsay asked. "Do you need something?"

"Need to say something." Her voice rasped but it held something of her old spirit. "I did you wrong, girl. At the wedding. Yelling at you like that. Shouldn't have."

Her words left Lyndsay stunned, but thinking about what Jenny had said yesterday, she answered, "If any forgiveness is needed, you have it."

"Plenty needed." Marnie's words came out rough and hoarse. "Not the best mother."

"No," Lyndsay agreed. "But I'm sure not the worst either."

The woman gasped for air and Lyndsay didn't want to tire her any further. She tucked her hand back under the sheet. "Rest now. All is okay."

Marnie's eyes slid shut.

Lyndsay watched her for a few moments longer while she processed the unexpected apology. Marnie had been wrong about some things, but Lyndsay herself had been too. They'd both made mistakes.

As she stood, Lyndsay let out a long breath, and some weight of anger, shame, and guilt left her along with the air.

●

When Lyndsay got back to the living room, the football game had ended and Aaron was hanging stocking hooks on the old mantel shelf. Jenny and her dad were working on dinner in the kitchen and Josh had been sent to town to pick up the printed pictures from yesterday's photo session in front of the tree.

"Tell me about becoming an architect," Aaron asked Lyndsay.

"Not that much interesting to tell. Got an undergrad degree in engineering, a masters in Architecture and had to do a year's internship. I just got my official license a few weeks ago."

"Congratulations. You worked hard for it."

"I did. Now I have to find a job where I can use it. But what are you doing these days?"

"Licensed general contractor. Mostly doing commercial construction."

They talked about jobs his company had done, including a warehouse for a major distribution firm and a new section of an upscale shopping center, until Josh returned and Jenny announced that dinner was ready. After dinner, they sat in the living room to listen to the final segment of *A Christmas Carol*.

"What a wonderful story," Lyndsay said, when Tom had read the last line, Tiny Tim's immortal words, "God bless us, every one." She looked at the others. "I love how transformative it was for him to see himself as others saw him and realize it wasn't what he wanted to be."

Then they hung the stockings Jenny had decorated with each person's name from the hooks on the mantel shelf, before heading for bed.

Heeding Jenny's advice, Lyndsay waited for an hour, while she checked email and texts, before creeping out to the living room with her gifts.

She scoped out the room but saw no one else, so she tucked a few small things into stockings and put the rest of her presents under the tree. She wasn't the first, and probably wouldn't be the last to visit the tree that night. She tiptoed back to bed oddly satisfied and happy over her first-ever Santa run.

•

They all woke earlier than normal and gathered in the kitchen for coffee and warm pastries. There, they discovered that an inch of snow had fallen overnight, covering everything with a fresh, white blanket.

As she ate her pastry, Lyndsay wondered if the others were as eager and excited to dig into the pile of presents under the tree as she was.

Before they exchanged gifts, Josh brought Marnie in and set her gently in the largest armchair, still wrapped in a blanket.

Marnie's strength wouldn't last long, so they pulled out her gifts first.

Her hands shook so badly, Josh had to help her unwrap most things—the warm socks from Tom, the pretty embroidered handkerchief from Aaron, a large, soft, fuzzy blanket from Jenny. Josh didn't assist Marnie in opening the present from Lyndsay and himself.

It took a while for Marnie's weak, unsteady hands to tear away the paper and open the box. She stared into it for a long moment—such a long time, that Lyndsay wondered if she was appalled by the picture of her and Josh inserted in a frame that said, simply, "Mother".

Marnie trembled. Her fingers tightened around the frame, and a tear ran down her sunken cheek. Her lips attempted a smile before she leaned back and closed her eyes.

"Do you want to go back to bed?" Josh asked.

Marnie shook her head in a bare negative.

Tom distributed the stockings and the rest of the presents. Lyndsay emptied her stocking, delighted by small boxes of tiny pastries, candy, fruit and nuts. She also unwrapped pretty hair pins, scented soap and hand cream. The others had similar things, with a more masculine slant for the men.

Lyndsay took her time unwrapping the other presents, while she watched the others with interest. She couldn't help staring at Aaron as he picked up a gift.

He pulled out a book from Tom, a murder mystery he said he'd been wanting to read. Then he lifted Lyn's gift. She watched as he opened the box with the plaid flannel shirt.

He looked pleased. "You must've had help from Josh, picking this out."

She nodded.

He pointed to a small box on her stack. "Now you have to open my gift."

She did and found a lovely silver bracelet with an engraved plate showing a building plan and draftsmen's tools. She gasped. "It's beautiful. But you didn't just walk into a store and pick this out."

"I had a co-conspirator," he admitted, nodding toward Josh.

With Aaron's help Lyndsay put the bracelet on.

Josh and Jenny gave her a beautiful cashmere sweater, and Tom had contributed a coffee table book of architectural drawings of famous buildings.

"These are amazing! Thank you so much, everyone," Lyndsay said.

Marnie was fast asleep in the chair, still clutching the picture. She didn't rouse when Josh picked her up to take her back to bed.

They all pitched in to produce a lavish, early dinner of roast turkey, stuffing, mashed white potatoes, sweet potatoes, green beans and dinner rolls, with an apple pie for dessert.

They lingered over the meal, eating until they were stuffed almost to bursting, then everyone helped with the clean up. When they were done, the refrigerator held enough leftovers to feed them all for several more days.

Josh looked in on Marnie afterward. He emerged a moment later and asked Lyndsay to come with him.

They both stopped in the doorway. Marnie was asleep, the picture they'd given her resting on her chest with her hand still clenched around it.

Tom was snoozing on the couch when they returned to the living room and Jenny had also disappeared.

Aaron asked if Lyndsay would like to take a walk outside.

They put on coats, hats and snow boots which Aaron unearthed from somewhere then headed out. Cold air smacked Lyndsay in the face, but the chill braced her, as well as making her shiver.

Aaron held her hand to help her down the steps and didn't drop it once they reached the ground. They turned to the driveway and walked down its length to the lightly traveled side road and continued along it.

The sun shone brightly now out of a clear blue sky, and a few birds twittered in the trees. The blanket of pure white snow made everything look fresh and clean and new. Her stomach fluttered with nerves and excitement.

Lyndsay said, "I talked to Marnie yesterday. I think she was actually trying to apologize."

"For the wedding?"

"And a lot of other things." She watched a squirrel scamper across the fresh snow.

"How did you respond?"

"I told her I forgave her. Jenny urged me to do it. I was reluctant at first, but I have to say, it was remarkably freeing. And now I have to apologize to you as well."

His sandy brows rose to almost meet the bottom of the stocking cap he wore. "For what?"

"For running away at the wedding and leaving you to handle all the explanations and all the anger. Leaving you with the embarrassment. I was so wrapped up in my own humiliation, it never occurred to me what I was doing to you. And for refusing to take your calls afterward."

"I didn't blame you for it."

"You should have," she said. "I was thoughtless."

He smiled at her, showing gorgeous dimples in each cheek. "We were both beyond rational thought. All that champagne. Can we agree to forgive each other for whatever we think happened there?"

"That's generous of you, and I'm okay with it."

"Good." He squeezed the hand he held. "You know, I felt even more guilty because I'd wanted to kiss you for so long and couldn't."

"Why not?"

"Because you were Josh's little sister and—best friend or not—he'd've beaten me to a pulp if I even looked at you sideways."

"And all those years I had a crush on you but thought you just saw me as your best friend's pesky sister."

He chuckled. "Sometimes you were that, too. But at our high school graduation, you were probably around fifteen, all dressed up and looking very grown up, and it hit me like a ton of bricks how beautiful you were. You smiled at me, and I was a goner." He sighed. "But I'd already enrolled in the army, so off I went, and then on to college. Josh and I kept in touch and saw each other around here occasionally, but I didn't see you again until his wedding. One look at you, and I realized it was all still there. All the feelings. That's really my only excuse for how I acted. That and the champagne."

"The champagne has a lot to answer for." She had a lot to answer for, too. Her own doubts and fear and humiliation had kept her from listening to him for far too long. Time to put that all behind her. "What would Josh think about us, now?"

"He knows how I feel about you, and he's okay with it. I suspect he thinks you have feelings for me, too."

"Josh has always known me pretty well."

"I may be jumping the gun here, but how hard would it be to get your architect's license in Massachusetts?"

"Probably not too hard." Her hand shook as she held her hat against a gust of wind. She dared to envision a better future, one that would include Aaron and all the excitement he roused in her heart. Maybe a thrilling partnership like Josh and Jenny had?

"Would you consider it?"

She looked at him, meeting his steady, intent gaze. "Yes. I don't know if I'm totally ready to make that leap yet, but I think I will be."

"We need time to get to know each other better. To date. To connect. We can arrange that. I feel pretty sure of my feelings, though."

He drew her into his arms. He kissed her until she was all but melting, right there in the middle of the road, with her feet getting cold in the boots but the rest of her body heating up with his warmth and the fire rousing inside.

After a while they drew apart and headed back to the house. "I wonder…" Lyndsay mused as they walked.

"What?"

"I know Jenny organized this whole weekend. Do you suppose she had this in mind? Bringing us back together?"

"Probably," he said. "Along with several other purposes. I think she first intended it primarily for Josh to reconcile with Marnie, then along the way, she realized you needed it, too, and it ballooned from there."

"Gave her father a place to come and be part of a family again," Lyndsay suggested. "You, too. Brought us together again. Helped Josh and I find peace with Marnie. Yeah, I think she saw this as a way to perform a lot of miracles in one beautiful holiday gathering."

Aaron's eyes shone with warmth and joy. "I'm glad to be part of the miracles. Christmas will always be a time of wonder for me now."

Lyndsay returned his smile. "I've never understood what Christmas spirit meant. It always seemed like just another day to sleep in late and maybe get some extra study in. It's all different now. It's in my heart. Just like you are."

Karen McCullough is the author of almost two dozen published novels and novellas in the mystery, romance, suspense, and fantasy genres, including the Market Center Mysteries Series and three books in the No Brides Club series of romance novels. A member of Mystery Writers of America, Sisters in Crime, and the Piedmont Authors Network, she is also a past president of the Southeast chapter of Mystery Writers of America and past member of the MWA National Board. Karen has won numerous awards, including an Eppie Award for fantasy, and has also been a finalist in the Daphne, Prism, Dream Realm, Rising Star, Lories, and Vixen Award contests. Her short fiction has appeared in a wide variety of anthologies. She lives in Greensboro, NC, with her husband of many years.

Visit Karen's Site: www.kmccullough.com

The Reunion

Annie Reed

December. What an odd time for a high school reunion.

Especially a twenty-*fourth* reunion. Why not just wait until next summer for their twenty-fifth?

Jeannie tucked her carry-on beneath the seat in front of her. The seatbelt latched around her newly trim hips with room to spare—if that wasn't proof positive that her revamped eating regime was doing its job, she didn't know what was—and she settled back to watch the plane take off from her window seat.

She didn't like flying all that much, but driving from her daughter's home in Arizona to her old hometown outside of Portland, Oregon, was prohibitive, especially in December.

"Too many mountain passes, Mom," Kristie had said. "You never know what they'll be like, this time of year." Unspoken, of course, was that Kristie didn't want her mom driving all that way alone.

Jeannie and her husband used to visit their daughter at least once a year, after Kristie moved to Arizona to go to college. Jake would take enough vacation time to let them drive the whole way. They'd spend a night in Las Vegas on the way down and a night in Reno on the way back. They'd treat themselves to dinner at a fancy restaurant, maybe catch a floor show in one of the casinos, and enjoy themselves while they took a break from all that driving.

The drive got shorter after Jake's company transferred him to Sacramento. That was the only thing Jeannie had liked about living in California. They'd made plans to move back to Oregon as soon as he retired.

Last January, he'd had a sudden and massive heart attack and

Jeannie had become a widow at forty-two.

Kristie had convinced her to come stay with her in Arizona, at least for a while. "I don't like the idea of you being alone in a place you don't like, Mom," she'd said.

Jeannie had reluctantly agreed. She didn't want to be a burden to her daughter. Kristie had a life of her own now, but Jeannie didn't want to be alone, either, while she tried to figure out what to do with the rest of her life.

Her work as a freelance graphic designer could be done anywhere with a stable internet connection. She and Jake had always lived wherever Jake's job took him. The idea that she could live anywhere she wanted now was hard to wrap her mind around.

After living for most of this year in Arizona, Jeannie had decided the desert southwest was a nice place to visit, but she didn't want to live there permanently. Kristie loved the desert and the heat. Jeannie missed cool weather and hills that were actually green.

Sacramento was out, as well. Jeannie had never really made friends of her own there. Just acquaintances she'd met through Jake's work. And the summers in Sacramento were not only almost as hot as Arizona, but humid.

Seattle was a possibility. She loved how green everything was in the Pacific Northwest, and she'd enjoyed the waterfront area, but she'd only been there once, with Jake when he'd had to attend a work-related conference. She didn't know anyone in Seattle, much less Washington state, and Seattle to Arizona was an even longer trip.

When Jeannie had received the invitation to her twenty-fourth high school reunion, it seemed like a sign. She'd been mulling over moving back to the town where she'd grown up. Her own parents were gone, now, but she had fond memories of the place. The reunion would allow her to see if her good feelings were only because it was where she'd met and fallen in love with Jake.

The one thing that made her hesitate was leaving Kristie so close to the holidays. Jeannie had been looking forward to creating new holiday traditions with her daughter, to make up for all the things she wouldn't be doing this year with Jake. Kristie had been training for months for a marathon she'd be running after the first of the year. Jeannie had adopted Kristie's healthier eating habits, which meant any new traditions wouldn't include baking the cookies they'd made when Kristie was little.

If she was being honest with herself, leaving Kristie behind was one of the things which made Jeannie hesitate about going to the reunion.

She hadn't recognized any of the names on the reunion committee, which reminded her that she didn't really know most of the people she'd gone to school with all that well. She'd only had one good friend in high school. Marta Gilroy had been another slightly overweight art nerd, like Jeannie. To say they hadn't fit in with the popular girls was an understatement.

Marta had been goth before the word became a fashion statement. She'd dressed in various shades of black and wore her black hair long and straight. While Jeannie had been quiet and shy, Marta had been loud and proud, with an incredibly wicked sense of humor.

Jeannie had lost track of Marta after they'd graduated. She'd been surprised to receive a heartfelt condolence card from Marta when Jake passed away. Marta had included her email address, along with a photograph of herself—still goth, still slightly overweight—next to a sign for a gallery showing of her art. The return address on the envelope was in New York City.

Since then, the two had corresponded through email. Marta had told Jeannie about the reunion. She'd said she couldn't afford a cross-country airline ticket, especially not with holiday prices for air travel. She told Jeannie she should go to make sure the artsy-fartsy contingent was well-represented.

Jeannie didn't want to go by herself to a reunion where she'd feel like a total outsider, but Kristie had encouraged her to go. "You can't hide out with me forever, Mom."

Was that what Jeannie had been doing? She went a few places by herself, but didn't interact with anyone. Some days, all she did was sit in

Kristie's living room and read. She'd begun to think she might want someone special in her life again, but that possibility was so far off in the future she couldn't imagine it.

Jeannie needed to find a place of her own, and unless she wanted to become the secretive widow all her new neighbors gossiped about, she'd have to force herself to go out among people again. So she'd emailed the reunion coordinator and said she'd be there.

Only now she was having second thoughts.

The lights inside the plane flickered and a thump vibrated the floor beneath her feet as the plane taxied away from the terminal. The low-level thrum of nerves which had been building in her since she'd lined up to board the plane settled into a tight little ball in her tummy, which made her glad she'd only had a light breakfast.

"Nervous flyer, dear?" the woman in the aisle seat asked. She was a generation older than Jeannie, with graying hair done in an attractive, tightly curled style which accented her delicate features.

Jeannie gave the woman a polite smile while she considered the question.

Was her nervous stomach telling her she was making a mistake? Should she ditch the reunion and take the next flight back to Arizona? But would she be able to face Kristie, much less look at herself in the mirror, knowing that just the idea of going to a party by herself for the first time in more than two decades had made her run away with her tail between her legs?

She didn't want to tell any of that to a stranger.

"It's been a long time since I've been on an airplane," she said instead. It wasn't a fib. The last time she'd been on a plane had been the trip to Seattle with Jake.

Jeannie looked out the window, and the woman took the hint. They could have spent the entire flight chatting, but Jeannie didn't feel up to polite conversation with a stranger. She'd be doing enough of that this weekend. *If* she decided to go to the reunion.

She still had time to decide whether that part of the trip would be a mistake.

●

Raymond had made a terrible mistake. He'd agreed to meet his cousin for coffee at a trendy new café but, of course, Lucas had an ulterior motive.

"Will you be my plus-one to the reunion? *Please?*" Lucas looked at Raymond with those puppy-dog brown eyes of his that he'd used to such great effect back when they'd still been kids.

Those eyes had got Lucas into—and out of—more trouble than a man had any right to get into. Especially a forty-three-year-old gay man who had his own successful clothing line and who, with his three business partners, owned three separate malls in the Portland area.

Raymond had brokered the deals on two of them.

"Can't you get a date?" Raymond asked.

Lucas sipped his skinny latte. "I'm not taking a date to my high school reunion. Are you crazy? I'd never hear the end of it. That's nearly as bad as taking a date to a wedding."

Lucas's mother—Raymond's aunt—was forever after the both of them to settle down. If Lucas took a date to the reunion, his mother would definitely get the wrong idea. He didn't have the temperament to stay with just one Mr. Right and raise a bunch of kids.

Raymond, on the other hand, thought he'd found the one Ms. Right he wanted to spend the rest of his life with. Unfortunately, after four years and one child, she'd found a more desirable Mr. Right. The divorce had left Raymond "emotionally scarred, sexually frustrated, and unwilling to get back in the saddle"—Lucas's description.

It had also left Raymond with a daughter he adored and didn't get to see nearly as often as he would have liked, especially after his ex moved to Tacoma. He had no desire to start a new relationship, only to risk losing it again. Emotionally scarred was one way of putting it. Gun shy was another.

Raymond sipped his holiday cold brew. "Why are you even going?" he asked Lucas. "You were miserable in high school."

Raymond was a couple of years older than Lucas and he'd gone to a different high school, where he'd achieved modest popularity, thanks to football. He'd still heard all about Lucas's teenage troubles, though. "There was only one person you even liked," Raymond said. An art student, if he recalled right, who'd been an outcast in her own way.

Lucas put his skinny latte on the little table where they sat, and looked at Raymond over the top of his purple-framed reading glasses. "Are you seriously asking me why I'm going?" He held his hands out wide, the better to show off a his flamboyant sportscoat, from his *Coat of Many Colors* line. "If you were as rich and successful and utterly fabulous as I am, wouldn't you want to rub it in all their snooty faces?"

Raymond had to admit that Lucas made a good point. Raymond had never felt like an outcast in high school, but he hadn't been as popular as the quarterback, either. "You know you're perpetuating a stereotype," he said.

Lucas chuckled. "All the better to mess with their heads. At least I'm not asking you to go in drag."

"Good God, no." Raymond stifled a sigh. He could either be a jerk and say no, or he could be a good friend. When he'd still been in shock over the divorce, Lucas had been there for him. What was one evening out of his life? It wasn't like he had any better offers.

"I'm not dancing with you," he said.

"Wouldn't expect you to," Lucas said.

"And we're not holding hands."

"That's fine."

"And no kissing!"

Lucas's mouth fell open in mock surprise. "Oh, no! Be still my heart." He tilted his head to one side, his expression suddenly serious. "So you'll go?" he said. "I don't want them to think I'm a sad, lonely gay man."

Puppy-dog eyes. Raymond always fell for it. "Okay, I'll go."

●

As Raymond stood next to Lucas at the door to the high school gym, uncomfortable in his brand-new suit, he realized he should have set one more condition before agreeing to be Lucas's plus-one.

He should have told Lucas he'd only go if he could wear his own clothes.

●

Jeannie stood by herself at the bar which had been set up at the far end of the gym, waiting for the bartender—*Jimmy Jones, Chess Club President,* his name tag read—to mix her rum and Diet Coke, light on the rum.

The reunion committee had done a decent job of decorating the gym, even though most of the decorations consisted of red, green, and white helium-filled balloons and crepe paper streamers. Round tables with butcher paper tablecloths and folding metal chairs were scattered across the gym floor. The lights had been turned down to a semi-intimate setting and a few couples were dancing in an empty space in the middle of the gym to a Boyz II Men rendition of a traditional Christmas carol.

Jimmy Jones, the barman, was dressed in a Santa Claus suit minus the beard. She didn't remember him. Of course, he probably hadn't been able to fill out a Santa suit with his own belly in high school.

"Here you go." He handed her a plastic cup holding her drink. He gave her an exaggerated wink and the unsexiest leer she'd ever seen, as their fingers briefly touched.

Jeannie's return smile was polite, but frosty.

Most of the single—and singularly unappealing—men at the reunion had hit on her at one time or another since she'd walked beneath the balloon-covered trellis into the gym. Thankfully no one had added mistletoe to the decorations, or she would have been in trouble.

She had no idea why men who surely didn't remember her any more than she remembered them were so attracted to her. She wasn't the prettiest woman at the reunion. That prize went to Cissy Henderson, former head cheerleader. Cissy was dressed in a gorgeous red party dress with a little Santa hat pinned to her short blonde hair. She had the same thin, lithe figure she'd had in high school.

Cissy had enveloped Jeannie in an enthusiastic hug, moments after Jeannie checked in at the front desk. Cissy had looked at Jeannie's name tag, first. She clearly had no idea who Jeannie was, but she'd hugged Jeannie hard just the same. Jeannie had been so surprised, she hadn't hugged back.

It had been that way all night. Women who hadn't given her the time of day in high school would peer at her name tag, then give her a huge hug and thank her for coming.

Between the hugs and the attention she was getting from the single men, Jeannie felt more than a little overwhelmed.

She missed Jake. She'd been doing well so far, driving her rental car around town, familiarizing herself with the some of her favorite restaurants and shops, like the art store where she and Marta had spent way too much of their free time, and marveling at the changes from nearly two decades of expansion to the downtown area. She'd even driven through older residential neighborhoods to see if there were any houses for sale that struck her fancy. She'd done all of it without feeling alone.

But now, surrounded by people she'd gone to school with, she felt like an outsider.

She would finish her drink and slip out. She doubted anyone would miss her.

"Didn't I tell you never to order a mixed drink in a bar?" came a familiar voice, from behind. "Bottled drinks you watch the bartender open, girlfriend."

Jeannie whirled, nearly spilling her drink. "Marta!"

Marta hugged her. Jeannie welcomed *this* hug with open arms.

"Surprised you, didn't I?" Marta said, when Jeannie finally let go.

"You lied to me!"

Marta gave her a rueful smile. "Not at the time. I really didn't think I'd make it, but then I sold a few pieces and *voila*! Here I am." She glanced around the room. "Is this party lame or what?"

From an adult point of view it was lame, but it was also wonderful—Marta was here! Marta, in a swirling black skirt, black, sequined blouse, and blue-black metallic extensions in her long, straight hair.

"Let's find a spot to sit and catch up," Jeannie said.

Marta took two steps toward the bleachers, then her mouth dropped open in surprise. "Would you look at that?"

Jeannie followed her gaze to the front of the gym. A handsome gay couple, dressed in coordinating holiday sports jackets—one burgundy red satin, the other forest green—stood just inside the balloon-covered trellis. The shorter of the two men looked vaguely familiar.

"Isn't that your friend…." Jeannie began. She couldn't remember his name, but he'd been the most flamboyantly gay student in their conservative school. Jeannie had been ignored, but he'd been tormented. Which meant that Marta, being the contrarian she was, had befriended him.

"Lucas!" Marta shouted.

Her bellow carried over the music—currently Celine Dion's version of *The Christmas Song*—and half the people looked in their direction. Marta didn't seem to care.

Lucas looked in their direction. A huge grin split his face. "Marta-farta!" he shouted back, waving frantically.

Jeannie couldn't help but notice that the man he was with looked as though he wanted to sink into the floor. If he was dating Lucas, he should be used to things like this.

Marta made a beeline toward Lucas. Jeannie trailed in her wake.

Lucas met them in the middle of the gym. He enveloped Marta in a bear hug that made all the hugs Jeannie had received look tame.

She tried not to stare at the man who'd come with Lucas. Up close, he was incredibly handsome. Tall, with dark hair cut short and a strong jaw and cheekbones to die for. In the dim light of the gym, Jeannie couldn't tell whether his eyes were dark blue or brown, but they looked kind.

Marta and Lucas were still hugging each other.

Jeannie held out her hand to Lucas's date and introduced herself.

"Do you know Marta too?"

She almost missed his reply.

What she felt when his hand touched hers wasn't a zing. She'd only experienced that once in her life, and that had been on her first date with Jake. But she felt a definite pull of attraction.

What, was she nuts? He was Lucas's date, which was clear from their outfits. A gay man who dressed in a green satin sportscoat for a high school reunion wasn't someone she should be attracted to.

She did catch his name. Raymond Ellis.

"I take it they're friends," he said with a grin, glancing at Marta and Lucas.

Jeannie tried to regain her composure, but her cheeks felt warm and she couldn't tone down her smile. She wondered if she'd held his hand too long. It had felt nice in hers.

"What gave it away?" she asked. "The nickname?"

"That was a clue," he said. "Lucas usually doesn't go around calling people 'farta.' At least, not that I know of."

"It is one of his tamer nicknames for Marta."

Jeannie went on to not only list all the wildly inappropriate names Lucas and Marta had once called each other, but also describe the reasons behind the most imaginative names. She trailed off when she realized she was babbling. Her unexpected attraction to a gay stranger had robbed her of what little people skills she had.

At least he looked amused. But was he amused at her, or at learning what his date had been like in high school?

"I'm sorry," she said. "I really shouldn't be allowed out in public. It's been a while since I've been to a social gathering. I should probably ask how long you've known Lucas."

"All his life," Lucas said, interrupting whatever Raymond had been about to say. He put an arm around Jeannie's waist and kissed her on the cheek, another thing no one had ever done to her in high school. "What say you and Marta grab a table, and Raymond and I get drinks?"

Jeannie began say she already had one—her barely touched rum and Diet Coke—but Lucas waved her off.

"That's just nasty," he said. "Let's get you a proper drink."

Marta gave Jeannie an odd look, then she glanced at Raymond. "I'll go with you to get the drinks," she said to Lucas. "I know what Jeannie likes and someone needs to protect you from bartender Santa. With that outfit, he might think you're one of his elves escaped from the toy factory."

"Santa's the one who'd need protecting." Lucas arched one brow in an exaggerated leer.

Marta held up a finger to Lucas in a *wait-a-second* gesture. Then she snagged Jeannie by the elbow and leaned in close to whisper in Jeannie's ear. "That's Lucas's cousin. A couple years older than us. Divorced. Father of one." She gave Jeanne's elbow a little squeeze. "And definitely *not* gay."

●

Of course, Raymond would meet the most beautiful woman he'd seen in ages while he was wearing a shiny green sportscoat that made him look like one of Santa's elves—a beautiful woman who'd bantered with him moments ago, but now looked as though she wanted to disappear with embarrassment. Whatever Lucas's friend Marta had whispered in her ear had thrown her for a loop.

Raymond wanted to get back to the place where they'd just been, that getting-to-know-each-other phase of a relationship which had the potential to go someplace special.

The fact that he'd even thought of the word "relationship" was miraculous, and almost as amazing as how perfectly her hand fit in his, and the way he couldn't tear his gaze from her. Apparently, his divorce hadn't ruined him for life, after all.

"Should we grab a table?" he asked her.

Jeannie glanced toward the bar.

Raymond followed her gaze.

A small crowd had gathered around Marta and Lucas, but no one seemed to be giving his cousin grief. Lucas had made his grand entrance, discovered at least one old high school friend, and now he'd hit his stride as his fabulously successful gay self.

That left Raymond free to find out if his unexpected attraction to Jeannie was one-sided or something she might want to pursue, too.

"Doesn't look like we're getting drinks anytime soon." Jeannie seemed to make an effort to smile at him, but her smile was thin, and didn't strike him as having any humor in it. "You could always have a sip of mine if you'd like, but I have to warn you it's diet," she added.

The words were friendly, but her tone was off.

What the hell had happened?

Then she surprised him by putting a hand on his arm. "I'm sorry," she said. "That didn't quite come out right. I'm terrible at this—flir... getting-to-know-you small talk."

Had she almost said *flirting*?

"I'm out of practice," she continued. "Then Marta...." She shrugged, her cheeks flushing an adorable shade of pink. "Can we pretend I didn't say that?"

He grinned. He couldn't help it. He felt as though he was actually back in high school, and the girl he'd been crushing on had agreed to go out on a date with him.

"I hang around with someone like Lucas," he said, "and you have to ask if I'm okay with conversational gaffes?"

Good lord, he'd just said "gaffes." She wasn't the only one out of practice at flirting.

Thankfully she just grinned back, instead of pointing out how pretentious he sounded. "I guess that goes without saying. So Lucas is your cousin?"

Ah ha. That was what Marta had whispered in her ear. Which meant.... He gave himself a mental head-slap. She'd thought he was Lucas's date! "I just agreed to keep him company. I should have told him I'd only come if I could wear my own clothes."

"And that's not...?" She took her hand from his arm to gesture at his sportscoat. The loss of her touch made him miss that simple connection. How long had it been since he'd felt this way with a woman? "No,

I don't keep a shiny green jacket in my closet," he said. "It's from Lucas's clothing line. He's a designer. A successful one, at least now. In high school, he was the school outcast."

She gave him a thoughtful look. "And you agreed to come for moral support? Not a lot of guys would do that."

Someone at a nearby table took a photo with their cell. The flash illuminated her face long enough to give him a good look at her eyes. They were the deepest blue. Intelligent, kind, and with a touch of bewilderment at the situation she'd found herself in.

"Did you come with Marta tonight?" He was pretty sure she was alone. No wedding ring on her finger (he'd looked), and no one striding over to hook a possessive arm around her waist. There was the possibility she was Marta's date, though.

"I didn't even know she was coming." Jeannie shrugged. "I was about to leave before she surprised me."

"Not having a good time?"

She gave him a long look and the kind of smile that let him know his interest in her was definitely reciprocated. "I am now."

●

Jeannie was having the time of her life. She'd been flirting—yes, flirting!—with Raymond for what seemed like hours. Marta and Lucas had brought back drinks, and the four of them laughed and chatted and teased each other while the reunion went on around them.

She felt like a teenager, only not the teenager she'd been in high school. She hadn't met Jake until after she'd graduated, when he'd been a mature man of twenty-five to her quiet and shy eighteen. Before Jake, her love life had consisted of a few sporadic dates, and one disastrous high school prom.

Her date had been a gangly boy with an inflated opinion of himself. When it became clear to him that she wasn't going to "put out," as he'd called it, he'd ditched her to go drinking with his buddies. She'd been mortified.

Marta hadn't gone to the prom. It didn't fit with her ultra-disinterested-in-anything-remotely-mundane persona. Jeannie'd had no one to talk to once her date abandoned her. She'd spent the night sitting by herself on the bleachers, waiting for her date to come back. Eventually she'd called her parents to come and pick her up.

If only she had met someone like Raymond in high school! No, that wasn't right. If she had met Raymond then, she wouldn't have married Jake, and she'd never regret being married to Jake. They'd had a wonderful life together, and one amazing daughter.

Was this what high school life had been like for the popular girls? An evening spent flirting with the most handsome man in the room? Someone who made her heart skip a beat when he looked at her as though she was the present he'd always wanted to find beneath his Christmas tree?

Then the evening got even better.

The background music switched to a soulful version of "I'll be Home for Christmas".

Raymond leaned back in his chair and closed his eyes. "I love this song."

"You gotta do it," Lucas said.

Raymond glanced at his cousin.

Lucas gestured with his head toward Jeannie and grinned.

"I gotta do it," Raymond agreed. He stood and held out a hand to Jeannie. "Care to dance?"

Jeannie shot a glance at Marta.

"Don't look at me, girlfriend," Marta said. "I don't dance."

"Oh, come on," Lucas said. "Everyone dances to a song like this. Don't the words just pull at your heart?" He put a hand over his own heart as if to emphasize the emotion. "Life's too short not to have a little fun."

Lucas stood and pulled Marta to her feet.

"Okay, fine." She sounded more like an exasperated mom than a woman about to go dancing. "Between your suit and my dress, we are going to look fabulous on the dance floor. But no groping, mister!"

"Trust me, Ms. Farta," Lucas said. "You don't have the parts I'd want to grope."

Off they went, leaving Raymond still standing with his hand out, waiting for Jeannie.

Well, what was she waiting for? She smiled and took his hand.

He was an amazing dancer. Nothing fancy, no moves that made her worry about not stepping on his feet, or tripping over her own. He put one hand on her waist and enfolded her other hand in his, tucking them against his shoulder.

They slow-danced close enough to almost touch. Having him so close was exhilarating and maddening at the same time. Jeannie wanted to be closer, to rest her head on his shoulder, close her own eyes and lose herself in the moment, but she wasn't sure she should make the first move.

Instead, she tilted her head so she could look at his face. Jake had been just a little bit taller than she was. Raymond was taller than that, yet leaning back to look at his face didn't feel awkward. It felt right.

"I've never danced to this song before," she said. "What did you mean when you said you 'just gotta'?"

His expression softened. "It's the lyrics. About making a promise to be home for Christmas, all the while knowing you can't." His eyes got a far-away look. "My family always traveled to my grandparents' house for Christmas. From right after school got out until right before New Year's Eve, we were always gone."

She couldn't tell from his expression whether that was a cherished memory or something he'd merely put up with. She was just fascinated with this glimpse into his childhood.

"It was fun when I was little," he said, "but once I hit high school and had a girlfriend? Not so much."

"You wanted to be with her at Christmas."

"To be honest, I was hoping for a holiday kiss under the mistletoe, which I see no one thought to include in these decorations." He arched a brow and gave her a wicked grin.

Her cheeks heated. Again. She hadn't blushed this much in one night since… well, since forever.

"Anyway," he said, "when I couldn't talk my parents into letting me stay home by myself, I made a tape. Singing this song for my girlfriend."

"You didn't!"

"I did. I wrapped it and put a big bow on it and gave it to her on the last day of school."

"Were you in chorus? Or choir?" She couldn't remember what the class had been called when she'd been in high school, but there had been some phenomenal singers at her school.

"I was a football player," he said. "And I can't carry a tune to save my life."

"Oh, no." Jeannie could imagine what his rendition of the song must have sounded like.

"Oh, yes."

His grin softened. The fact that he was looking back at his teenage self with fond amusement said a lot about his character. This was a man who was comfortable enough in his own skin to be amused rather than embarrassed at his teenaged romantic gesture.

"I think she burned the tape after she listened to it, but it must have done the trick. After we got back home after Christmas, we… uh…." Now he *did* look embarrassed. "Are you sure you want to hear this part?"

He could tell her all about his silly teenage antics, but he was embarrassed to tell her he got lucky?

"I think I can fill in the blanks." She grinned at him. "So now you feel compelled to dance every time you hear the song?"

"Dancing to this song lead to the blank spot you just filled in." He moved her hand a little closer to his heart. "And no matter what Lucas thinks, I don't feel compelled to dance to it every time. Only when I have the right partner."

Oh.

Oh!

The nervous flutter she'd been feeling since she first touched his hand expanded to fill a spot in her heart she hadn't realized she'd been missing quite so badly. Jake had been her first true love, but he was gone. He wouldn't want her to spend the rest of her life alone and lonely. He'd want her to find a good man. Someone like Raymond? Quite possibly.

She closed the distance between them so she could rest her head on his shoulder. He wrapped his arm around her shoulder. He felt so solid, warm, and wonderful, she wondered why she hadn't done this sooner.

They danced with her head on his shoulder, both of them barely moving with the music, as "I'll be Home for Christmas" faded and another slow holiday song took its place.

She felt like she'd just found the best Christmas present ever under her tree. She didn't want this evening to end, which was amazing, considering she'd almost ditched the reunion not five minutes before Raymond had walked through the balloon-covered archway into the gym.

"I'm so glad I decided to come tonight," she said with a happy sigh. "I almost didn't, this close to Christmas."

"Being here with you tonight, it's the best Christmas present I've had in a long time, " he said. "There's a lot of that going around. Lucas said the committee is ecstatic so many people turned out for Cissy."

What an odd thing to say. Reunions were about everyone in the class, not just the head cheerleader. Was that why Cissy had hugged Jeannie like they were long-lost friends, because she thought the party was just for her?

"I don't understand," Jeannie said. "What does Cissy have to do with anything?"

Raymond tilted his head to look at her. His comfortable smile faded. A faint line of concern built between his brows. "You don't know?" he asked.

"Know what?"

His arm tightened around her shoulder, as if to give her support. "She's had it pretty rough the last year. From what Lucas told me, her health isn't good. Going to her twenty-fifth high school reunion gave her something to focus on, but there's a chance she might not be around next summer to enjoy it."

Jeannie stopped dancing. Her feet just wouldn't move.

That explained so much. Why this reunion was their twenty-*fourth* and why it was being held so close to Christmas. Why Cissy had held on so tight when she'd hugged Jeannie, a virtual stranger. And why all the once-popular girls had been so happy Jeannie was here. It wasn't about their reaction to seeing Jeannie again, it was about giving their friend the one thing she really wanted.

"It's their Christmas gift to her," she murmured.

●

Raymond hated breaking such bad news to Jeannie.

She had one of the kindest hearts he'd ever encountered. Maybe because he dealt in the cutthroat world of real estate, he'd gotten used to the idea that all the women he would ever meet would be hard and jaded, but Jeannie wasn't that way.

She'd told him about her marriage and how it had ended out of the blue when her husband passed away. He hadn't suffered, she'd said, but Raymond could tell she was still getting over the loss. That was why he'd put space between them when he took her onto the dance floor, when all he really wanted to do was hold her tight and never let go.

He couldn't remember ever feeling this way about a woman before, not even his ex-wife. Sure, he'd loved her—how could he not? She'd given him his wonderful daughter. But this was different. He'd never believed in love at first sight. Attraction, yes. Lust? Absolutely. He still remembered how he'd felt as a teenager, learning to cope with an overload of hormones.

His feelings for Jeannie were totally different. She was warm and wonderful, soft and feminine and absolutely, totally beautiful. He could imagine making a life with this woman. If this wasn't love, he didn't know what was.

And now he'd ruined everything.

"Will you excuse me for a moment?" she asked.

She left without waiting for him to reply. He had an idea she was going to see Cissy, but he didn't know Cissy. Even if Jeannie had invited him along, it would have made the moment awkward, so he went back to the table.

Marta was sitting by herself, sipping her drink. She'd switched to plain soda two drinks ago, claiming she had an early flight and the last thing she needed was a hangover.

"She ditch you on the dance floor?" Marta gave him a weary smile. She'd complained earlier about jet lag, and he guessed the time difference had finally caught up to her.

He shrugged and sat down. He must have looked dejected because she reached over and patted his arm. "Don't worry. She'll be back."

"I made a mistake and told her about Cissy. Finding out an old high school chum's only got a few months to live…if that's not a mood killer, I'm not sure what is." He sounded whiny, even to himself. If Lucas was here, he'd give Raymond all sorts of shit.

"They weren't chums," Marta said. "In fact, I was her only friend. We lost touch over the years, but you know what? I don't think I've ever seen her as happy as she's been tonight. Have a little faith."

He gave her his own weary smile. He hadn't felt tired at all on the dance floor. He'd been energized. Alive in a way he hadn't in a really long time.

Marta pulled her hand back. "I probably shouldn't mention this, but you're in real estate, right? Lucas said you brokered deals for him, when he was going on and on about his fashion lines."

Raymond nodded.

"Jeannie's thinking about relocating, and she's been looking at houses. By herself."

His heart skipped a beat. Jeannie might be moving here?

"She'll be in town for the rest of the week." Marta leaned back in her chair with a self-satisfied grin. "I bet she'd like some company."

"Are you playing matchmaker?"

"It's Christmas," she said. "Everyone deserves a bit of good cheer."

•

Jeannie found Raymond sitting at their table with Marta, who just barely stifled a yawn.

"Damn, I hate to admit I'm getting old," Marta said, "but I can't party like I used to."

"You never partied," Jeannie said.

"You didn't know me in college." Marta stood and stretched her back, then held her arms wide. "Give me a hug and tell me it won't be another twenty-four years before we see each other again."

Jeannie gave her high school buddy an enthusiastic hug. "I promise," she whispered in Marta's ear. "You sure you have to take that flight tomorrow?"

"One day turnaround. All I could manage." Marta gave her a squeeze then let her go. "I came all this way to see you. So maybe it's your turn to come and see me." She shot a sideways glance at Raymond, then gave Jeannie a grin. "If you're not too busy."

Raymond snorted, which he covered with a hand over his mouth.

What had they been talking about? Jeannie hadn't been gone all that long. She'd just wanted to give Cissy another hug—a proper one this time—and to wish her well. Cissy had been surprised, but seemed genuinely happy, if tired. Jeannie hadn't pried into Cissy's health, but it was clear that as much as the reunion had energized her earlier, it was draining her now. She'd probably leave soon.

Jeannie should leave, too. She had a full day of house-hunting planned for tomorrow. Before she left, though, she wanted one more dance with Raymond.

She held out her hand to him. "Care to dance?"

He took her hand and led her to the dance floor. "Jingle Bell Rock" wasn't a song to slow dance to, so she held his hands instead of leaning her head on his shoulder.

"What were you two conspiring about?" she asked.

"Houses," he said. "I hear you might be in the market for a house."

She'd be lying if she said she hadn't considered moving back here might mean she could keep seeing Raymond. Which was silly. They'd just met. There was no guarantee he'd want to see her after tonight.

"I could show you some possibilities," he said. "Officially, of course."

Officially?

"I'm a real estate broker," he said in answer to her unasked question.

They'd never talked about what they did for a living. They'd chatted about high school and flirted with each other, and listened while Lucas and Marta bantered back and forth. What were the odds that she'd meet a wonderful man who would not only steal her heart, but help her find a new home?

"Can you start tomorrow?" she asked, with a hopeful, happy smile.

He pulled her in close. "Tomorrow sounds like a plan."

She wanted to kiss him, but she felt as though he'd been holding himself back all evening. She hoped that all he needed was a little push. She reached in the pocket of her slacks and pulled out a sprig of plastic mistletoe she'd spotted on one of the tables.

She couldn't quite hold the sprig over his head—he was a little too tall for that—but she did her best. "Look what I found."

A slow smile spread over his face. "I do believe that's mistletoe."

"I do believe," she echoed. "It's not 'I'll be Home for Christmas,' but it's the best I could do on short notice."

His glance fell to her mouth, then lifted back to her eyes. "It might be time to start a new tradition." He lowered his lips to hers.

The world melted away as they shared a tender kiss beneath the plastic mistletoe. It had been a long time since Jeannie had been kissed so sweetly.

She knew this would be the first of many kisses she would share with this man. They'd see each other tomorrow and maybe the day after that. They'd get to know each other better than they had tonight.

But tonight had taught her one thing she'd allowed herself to forget while she was living with her daughter. Life was short. Second chances didn't come around often. Cissy's friends had moved an entire reunion to make sure Cissy got a second chance to experience high school.

Meeting Raymond was giving Jeannie a second chance at love. She wouldn't squander it.

When their lips parted, she stared into Raymond's eyes.

Kind eyes, she'd thought earlier. *Loving eyes,* she thought now. "Tradition implies we'll be doing that more often."

He stroked the side of her face with one strong, gentle hand. "You can count on it."

Count on it? Oh yes, she most definitely would.

A prolific, versatile, and award-winning writer, Annie Reed's written more short fiction than she can count. She's a frequent contributor to both *Fiction River* and *Pulphouse Fiction Magazine.* Her stories appear regularly on Tangent Online's recommended reading lists, and "The Color of Guilt," originally published in *Fiction River: Hidden in Crime,* was selected as one of *The Best Crime and Mystery Stories 2016* (another one of her stories, "The Flower of the Tabernacle," also received an Honorable Mention). She's even had a sweet holiday romance story selected for inclusion in study materials for Japanese college entrance exams. Her *Unexpected* series of short-story collections showcase some of the best of her work.

Annie's a founding member and contributor to the innovative Uncollected Anthology series of themed urban and contemporary fantasy anthologies. She writes romance, mystery, science fiction, and fantasy under her own name and suspense novels as Kris Sparks. She also writes sweet romance novels under the name Liz McKnight. *Sweet Valentines,* an anthology of sweet holiday romance stories which Annie edited, will be released in early 2022.

Visit Annie's site: www.anniereed.wordpress.com

Burying His Ghost of Christmas Past

Tracy Cooper-Posey

If someone had predicted, last Christmas Day, that this time next year, Narelle would be sitting on a beach, sipping champagne and wriggling her bare toes in warm sand, she would have laughed at them.

Yet here she was.

Only, it wasn't Bora Bora or the Maldives, or some other packaged resort with palm trees. Western Australia didn't come with palm trees, unless they were planted deliberately.

But the beach sand was bone white, the sun was dazzling. The water was...oh, it was everything she remembered! Green at the edges, shifting to turquoise blue, and so still and clear that the corrugated sand at the bottom gleamed in the sun. There wasn't a skerrick of seaweed anywhere. Farther out, the water deepened to dark blue, and the low humps of waves rose gently.

At the end of the shallow bay, the headland of sharp red rocks thrust into the warm air. The water was choppy there, churning over the reef that surrounded the headland. She'd walked upon that reef many times...a long time ago.

"Mom!" Dylan shouted. It sounded as though it wasn't the first time he'd called.

Narelle sat up carefully, so her champagne didn't spill. The backs of her legs were damp against the fabric of the folding chair. Seven in the morning and it was already warm enough to swim. "What is it, Dylan?"

Her oldest son slogged through the sand to where she was sitting with the other women while the men set up the barbecue—which was nothing more than a grill resting on rocks over a fire.

Dylan was seventeen and would graduate high school in June. At home, he was full of swaggering young adult confidence. He didn't look so sure of himself now. "They don't have coffee, mom! I'm gonna get a headache if I don't get coffee. That stuff on the plane was gross."

"There will be tea later. You'll feel better when you've had breakfast." She gave him a smile. "We talked about how different it would be, remember? This is just part of the difference."

Dylan wore long bathing shorts and nothing else, but unlike the other children here, his chest was very pale. All her kids looked washed out and white. A few days in the Australian sun would fix that.

Her son looked around the beach, scanning the people moving across the sand, making drinks, preparing food, chatting and laughing, building fires and even more drinking. Most of the local kids were already in the water, doing handstands, shallow diving, floating and splashing each other.

Narelle had never got around to taking her kids to swimming lessons. Hockey and football and soccer had filled their days. "Why don't you paddle at the edge of the water?" she suggested.

Dylan looked at the water doubtfully. "There's just…*so* many people!" he breathed. His voice lowered as he added, "They're really all your family?"

"Many of them," Narelle said, trying not to laugh. "And they're your family, too." Her kids were really out of their element here. "Some of them live in the houses we passed when we drove from the airstrip last night. Do you remember?"

"Along the track with the potholes?" Dylan said. "Those houses are all part of the farm?"

"Station. Yes. All the families from those houses are here, too. They're station hands and workers and they're joining the big house for Christmas Day." She added gently, "Not everyone is here yet, either." Marion Williams and her family had not arrived, although they were expected. Marion…and Dane.

Dylan rubbed his temple with a motion that reminded Narelle sharply of his father. "I need coffee," he grouched.

"They're making billy tea," she assured him, as she spotted one of the men scooping a handful of loose tea into a can with a wire handle. "That will more than make up for no coffee." She remembered the bitter taste and the caffeine kick, and her mouth watered. It had been too long since she'd drunk tea that strong. Tea bags just weren't the same.

"*Billy* tea?" Dylan sounded offended. Then he added, "More differences?"

"More differences," she confirmed.

He turned on one heel and trudged toward the water. Emily, Julian and Harper stood close together, watching their big brother. He murmured something and all four moved hesitantly toward the water.

Jenny leaned toward Narelle. "Poor darlings! They look lost."

"They'll reorient quickly enough," Narelle said firmly, hoping it was true.

"Breakfast will help. You guys must be flat out buggered after the flight." Her sister glanced over at the plastic folding table where the breakfast supplies were being added. She squinted against the bright sun. "Garlic marinated prawns, bacon, lamb chops, fruit salad…and champagne, 'course." She held out her glass toward Narelle. "It's so good to have you back for Christmas."

Narelle clinked her glass against Jenny's, but didn't drink. She knew how much drinking happened throughout a typical Christmas Day in her family. She had to pace herself.

"Ah! There's Marion and Dane, finally," Jenny glanced up at the hard-packed dirt where everyone parked their utes, station wagons and four-wheel drives.

Narelle gripped her champagne glass. She didn't look up at the parking area, but her heart still jumped about.

You're stronger than ever, she reminded herself. *Time to end this. You're here to bury ghosts, Narelle Kelly.*

She sipped her champagne steadily as she listened to the men around the fire pit call out greetings to the new arrivals. The light, high voice was Marion Williams, Dane's mother. She still sounded opinionated, even though she was in her seventies.

When Narelle heard Dane's deep voice, giving a laconic answer to the questions thrown at them as they descended to the beach, invisible fingers rippled down her spine. She shivered, despite the warmth of the morning.

She frowned at the bubbles in her glass. She was over the man, damn it! Shivering at the mere sound of his voice wasn't part of being over him. It was just nerves, she decided. She had come a long way for the moment which was about to happen.

Deliberately, Narelle got out of her chair, let her sarong swing back around her knees, adjusted her sun hat and took off her sunglasses, ready to greet the new arrivals.

Marion Williams came toward her, her arms out and an enormous smile brightening her faded features. "Elly-nelly!! You're here! Oh, this is so *wonderful!*"

Narelle was enveloped in Marion's arms, as the older woman hugged her hard. Then Marion stepped back, her hands still on Narelle's arms. She sighed. "You've done *so* well for yourself. A best-selling author! You know, the last time we were in Perth, your books were all stacked up at the front of Angus & Robertson! I wanted to grab everyone walking past and tell 'em, 'hey, I know this author'!"

Narelle could feel her cheeks heating. "You're so sweet, Marion. Thank you."

Marion patted her arms, then looked around. "Where is he? Dane! Before you start telling everyone how to cook the lamb chops, come and say hello." The order was given in the same commanding voice Marion had used for years to direct the station hands. It hadn't lost any of its strength.

Narelle made herself look at Dane. She lifted her chin. Held her gaze steady.

Dane was speaking to Narelle's father, Joe, about something which made her father laugh in his soft, reticent way. Even viewed from behind, it seemed to Narelle that Dane had barely changed. Still tall, still rangy, but with strong shoulders that came from lifting heavy things—sheep, calves, hay bales, full seed bags, jerry cans and more. His hair was still dark, with the waves that always made it looked uncombed.

Narelle drained the last of her champagne as Dane turned slowly and headed in their direction.

"Here, let me take care of that," Jenny said, whipping the glass out of Narelle's hands, which left her with nothing to squeeze.

The women were only sitting a dozen feet away from the fire pit, but it might have been the length of a football field away. Narelle watched Dane move across the sand, a small, polite smile on his face. It seemed to her that it took forever for him to reach them, while her gaze slid over him, absorbing the details. The differences.

He'd grown older, of course. He'd be in his mid-forties now, but there didn't seem to be any grey in his hair. Nor in the well-trimmed stubble on his chin and around his mouth.

His eyes! They always seemed to be permanently narrowed against the sun—and he never wore sunglasses. There were crow's feet at the corners. They were new, but not at all disagreeable. It made it seem as though he smiled a lot.

Finally, he stopped in front of her. His gaze flicked over her, from top to bottom, and back. His smile shifted. Broadened a little. "Narelle Kelly, back home and covered in glory."

She managed to speak without her voice quivering. "Hello, Dane." It came out cool and polite, because of the tight control. Then she made the mistake of looking into his eyes.

They were green, warm and unwavering. She remembered staring into them, when she was much younger. They had made her feel then exactly the way she was feeling now. Her stomach tightened, while her heart zoomed, making her feel giddy.

"Our own best-selling writer. Fancy that." Marion's voice was full of pride.

"One who just signed a three-million-dollar contract for her next book," Dane said, in his slow, deep, honeyed voice. His gaze did not let her go. "The toast of New York," he said softly. "Well done, Ellie."

Ellie.

Narelle swallowed. Her heart would not slow down. She was trembling. All at once she recognized that the entire return-home-and-bury-the-past project had failed completely. She wasn't over him at all. Now he stood before her, she was almost ill with the power of her reaction to him.

What was she supposed to do next?

"Thank you," she managed to say, without betraying the true depth of her despair and her confusion…and how much she really wanted to slide her fingers through his hair, or rest her hand against his powerful chest. She could see the strip of tanned skin peeping between the open top buttons of his denim shirt.

Suddenly, a memory crashed back into her mind. Her lips against his heated skin…. She could remember exactly what he had tasted like. Smelled like.

"You haven't changed a bit." Dane's voice was tinged with approval.

"Don't be silly, Dane," Jenny said, pushing a full glass of champagne into Narelle's hand. "If you saw her on Hay Street in Perth, you wouldn't recognize her."

"That's just city polish," Dane said, his voice low. "The real stuff inside…that's still pure Narelle." His eyes would *not* let her go.

Narelle tore her gaze away from Dane, and looked at Jenny, instead. "We're all a lot older," she admitted.

"Older and better," Jenny said firmly.

"*Much* better," Dane agreed, his voice rumbling in Narelle's ears and her mind, making her trembling worsen.

Oh god, what was she going to do now?

●

There was enough breakfast to satisfy even *her* teenage kids' appetites and none of it was weird enough to make them stop eating. All four were damp and sandy, and ate enormously, which pleased Narelle in a distant way.

She barely ate, herself. She had no appetite at all, not even for the barbecued mullet fish. The older kids had carefully walked out over the reef around the headland and dug them up with short crow bars. They had once been her favourite Christmas breakfast indulgence.

Dane sat on the other side of the group of adults sitting in folding chairs, eating, drinking and laughing between every mouthful. Each time he spoke, Narelle's middle jumped. He didn't speak often. Dane never did. That was a blessing in disguise.

Narelle badly wanted to be by herself, somewhere behind a closed door, so she could pull herself together and put on an unconcerned face. How soon before someone noticed her falling apart because Dane Williams had spoken and smiled at her? He had been the only one on the station who knew about her new book deal, too. He had to read the publishing industry newsfeeds, to know that. No announcements had been made beyond the specialist trade sources.

When the daily rain clouds were spotted scudding across the pale blue sky toward them, everyone packed up swiftly, piled everything into the cars and headed back to the station, while still laughing and talking, trading insults and jeers and challenges, teasing each other and having a wonderful time even while working hard.

She had missed this easy banter! Even though she didn't have the heart to participate, herself, listening to the jokes and the cackles of laughter made the corner of her mouth lift up.

Narelle spread her kids out among the vehicles, for there wasn't room for all of them, her, and both her parents in the one station wagon. Narelle watched Dylan climb into the back of one of the utes and sit with his back against the rear window, his knees up and his arms relaxed against them. He didn't seem to be missing his coffee anymore.

It was a thirty-minute drive to the homestead, along rough, gravel tracks. The convoy lifted a cloud of pale brown dust into the sky for kilometers behind them for there was not a breath of wind.

When they reached the homestead, everyone unpacked, then headed to the main house. Her parents' house was a huge, old building on high stilts, with deep, shady verandahs on every side. A wide set of steps reached them. At the top of the steps, everyone ducked under the pink, red and yellow bougainvillea vines hanging over the edge of the verandah roof.

"Time for presents!" her mother called, opening the French doors into the big main room of the house.

They all crowded into the room to find chairs or a piece of floor where they could sit while opening their gifts. Seven children lived on the station, in the ringers' houses, and there were Narelle's kids, too. Their spiralling excitement over presents distracted the adults and gave Narelle a private moment to breathe deeply and command herself to relax.

Outside, the rain began—a hissing sheet of water which thundered on the corrugated iron roof and sent up reddish brown splashes of dirt in the yard outside.

Everyone who counted themselves family had gifts under the tree for Narelle and for each of her children—a thoughtfulness that touched her. None of the other children were overlooked, either, and soon the big, worn, comfortable room was adrift in crumpled Christmas wrapping.

"Oh, and I'm dying for you to open this one," Jenny said, hefting a large gift in both arms as she carried it over from the tree. She put it on Narelle's lap. "Go on."

"Lord, it's heavy!" Narelle said, steadying the big box on her knees. She slipped the card out from under the teal-colored ribbon, which just happened to be her favourite colour.

To Narelle. From Dane.

There was nothing else in the card but the workmanlike acknowledgement.

Narelle looked up, her heart hammering just like the rain on the roof. Dane *was* watching her, his head tilted a little to one side, his eyes narrowed. He was sitting on the carpet by the tree, one arm resting on a bent knee, the other on the ground, propping him up.

"Um…thank you, Dane," Narelle said awkwardly.

"Open it first. *Then* thank him," Jenny urged, pushing at Narelle's knee with her own. "You might hate it."

Narelle tugged the ribbon undone. It was real satin ribbon, not the paper gift-wrapping stuff. She pulled aside the paper and opened the cardboard box.

Another box was sitting inside. It was made of polished wood, a deep red colour, and etched glass.

"Wow…!" Jenny breathed, as Narelle lifted it out of the box. Jenny removed the cardboard carton and Narelle settled the wooden box on her knees. She ran her fingertips over the polished, glowing wood.

Through the glass lid, she saw a row of books. A long row. There was space at the end of the box for more, though.

The rest of the room had grown silent. Even the kids were watching her, now. Narelle tried to ignore the stares as she carefully opened the box.

"You bought books for an author, Dane?" Narelle's mother called.

"Not just any books," Jenny said, for she was close enough to see the spines. "They're all Narelle's books."

"Like she doesn't have enough of them, already!" Narelle's father said, and chuckled.

Narelle lifted the first book out. *Demon Cove,* the very first book she'd ever published. She opened it to check the copyright page. "These aren't just any books," she told her father. "These are first editions."

"Australian first editions," Dane said. "I guessed you didn't have those."

"I don't," Narelle admitted. Her voice was hoarse. She ran her fingers along the spine. They were all there. Every single one. Dane must have bought all of them the moment they were released. These were not used editions he'd found in a second-hand bookstore, somewhere in the city. None of the spines had been cracked. They were in mint condition.

Her hand shook as she returned *Demon Cove* to the box. It slid in neatly. The box had been tailored for the books.

"Well, a box of books isn't much of a present, even if they are first thingamajigs," her father declared.

Narelle lifted her head, expecting Dane to defend himself. Dane had never been afraid of her tall, rangy father, the way the ringers and station hands often were.

Dane had gone. The spot by the tree was empty.

Almost drowned by the heavy rain came the soft sound of the fly-wire kitchen door closing. The hinges *still* groaned, nineteen years later.

Narelle put the box on the ground. "I'd better…I'm just…" She couldn't think of anything polite to add to that. Instead, she hurried into the kitchen and out through the flywire door, which squeaked again.

Dane stood at the front of the verandah, his hands on the wide balcony railing, watching the rain fall. The overhanging eaves and the bougainvillea meant none of the rain reached the verandah. It fell in a steady shower, two feet away from him.

Narelle moved right up to him. The stew of feelings and jumbled thoughts drove her to speak directly. "You have to take those books back. I can't accept them."

Dane glanced at her, then away. "They're a gift. You don't give back gifts."

"They're…god, Dane, they're irreplaceable! You bought them all as they came out. You *must* have. It takes years to build a collection like that. I can't take them!"

"I want you to have them." His voice was low and hard. His gaze stayed on the muddy yard, and her mother's ailing flower garden.

She didn't know where the anger came from. Narelle gripped his arm. "Look at me, dammit!"

He didn't just look at her. He turned his whole body toward her… and she was already far too close. Was that how it happened? For she found herself leaning through the narrow space between them and pressing her lips to his.

It was a pathetic excuse for a kiss, but it didn't remain that way. With a groan, he pulled her against him. The kiss deepened. He thrust his hands into her hair and held her head steady and leaned over her and….

Narelle sighed into his mouth. This, she remembered. She hadn't, until just now. How had she made herself forget his touch? His kisses were heady, stronger than any champagne.

Narelle realized she was clinging to him only when he gripped her arms and thrust her away from him. He held her there, as if he was afraid she might try to move back close if he released her. He shook his head, his jaw working. "Don't you understand? I'm trying to *let you go*. Take the damn books, Narelle. Take them so I can…" He paused, as if he was suddenly aware of what he was about to say and halting with supreme effort.

He let go of her arms. Stepped back.

Then he spun and strode to the wide steps down into the yard, and hurried down them, the rain instantly soaking his shirt and making the shoulders turn dark blue.

Narelle leaned against the railing, dizzy. Her heart wouldn't stop strumming. Her body, either. But in her gut, she felt the same swirling sickness which had gripped her on the beach.

"Oh, shit…" she breathed. Something that sounded suspiciously like a sob tried to escape her and she clapped her hand over her mouth to hold it in.

"Narelle?" Jenny's voice was raised. She was in the kitchen.

Narelle drew in a shaking breath, grasping for calm, for a neutral expression, before Jenny came outside.

The door squeaked and slapped closed. "Dane isn't out here?"

"He went out into the rain." Despite her best efforts, Narelle's voice was bodiless. "And into the stable."

Jenny settled her hip on the balcony railing, next to Narelle. She raised a brow at her. "You scared him off?"

"I…" Narelle didn't have the strength to prevaricate. The words wouldn't come. "Yes," she said flatly.

Jenny gazed at the stable, on the other side of the muddy yard. "He never did talk much. After you left, he stopped talking pretty much altogether."

Narelle shook her head. "Don't tell me he mourned or something stupid like that." She crossed her arms, to hold in the pain. "He left me at the altar, near enough! The *day before the wedding*!"

"I know," Jenny said calmly. "I was there. And I was here for what came after you left, too."

"He married my bridesmaid barely six months later. He didn't miss me for long, huh?"

"Seems to me, you didn't wait too long to get married, yourself." Jenny's voice was still calm.

Yet Narelle still jumped, guilt stabbing her. "And I paid for it," she said honestly. "You know that thing about marrying in haste, yaddah yaddah?"

Jenny's gaze was calm. "It took you four kids to work out you'd married on the rebound?"

Narelle hung her head. "Eddie was having an affair. With my editor." She gripped the railing.

"Jeez… I'm sorry. I didn't know that."

"I didn't tell anyone," Narelle admitted. "Too embarrassed."

"Why? Affairs happen all the time."

"He wasn't just screwing her, it turns out," Narelle said. It was easier to watch the rain than look at her big sister. No wonder Dane had stared at it so hard. "He was also screwing me, too. He was my agent, and he was diverting money into an offshore account I didn't know about." She closed her eyes.

"Lordy, Narelle…!" Jenny's hand came down on her shoulder. "You've been through shit, haven't you?"

"And came out the other side," Narelle said, her voice hoarse. "I found another publisher. By myself. And I brokered the deal by myself."

"The three million deal that Dane spoke about?"

"That one, yeah." Narelle drew herself upright and made herself look at Jenny. Her sister watched her, sympathy in her eyes. "I figured I'd put the past behind me in New York, so it was time the do the same here."

"I thought you'd come here for Christmas," Jenny said.

"Christmas *is* the reason I came here. It's the one reason I can come here and not explain why."

One of the big doors on the stable swung open. Dane, sitting on her father's stallion, *Blue Streak,* emerged back out into the rain. He'd donned wet weather gear and her father's Akubra, the brim pulled low over his eyes.

Behind him, one of the blue heeler working dogs trotted, his tail up, eager for a run.

Dane didn't look at the house. He turned the stallion and galloped down the road, heading north. The horse's hooves splashed with each step.

"I guess the past doesn't want to be put away so easily, here," Jenny said, her tone thoughtful.

●

The rain stopped around three that afternoon. The clouds broke apart, letting in better light. But they didn't depart altogether.

A tiny breeze blew, bringing relief from the humid heat.

Christmas dinner was always held on the verandah, because there was no table, or multiples of tables, which could seat everyone, inside the house. There were nearly thirty people eating together.

Plank tabletops were put on trestles on the longest side of the verandah, and cloths laid over them. Chairs, crates and gum tree stumps were placed around the table as seating.

The men cooked breakfast, therefore the women cooked dinner, although most of it had been prepared well in advance. Narelle's mother was well practiced at orchestrating the Christmas Day dinner. It was a feast by anyone's measure. Roast chickens, *three* of them, roast ham, roast beef. Baked potatoes, with oodles of piping hot gravy, peas, cauliflower and cheese casserole, fresh, crunchy bread, stuffing, more vegetables steaming in tureens, and lots of sauces and condiments, including horseradish for the beef and mustard for the ham.

Growing up, Narelle had often suggested that on one of the hottest days of the year, a less traditional meal would be welcomed, but her family argued right back. They liked the old-style Christmas meal.

And they still did, apparently.

Narelle settled her children around the table, explained what was in the dishes they didn't recognize and urged them to try everything. She carefully didn't look down the long table to where Dane was sitting next to his mother. He'd returned to the house an hour ago, sliding through the door and settling in a chair as if he'd never left the room.

Narelle hadn't spoken to him since, but she'd grown jumpy and distracted. She'd hurried into the busy kitchen to volunteer, rather than sit where she could see him.

"Mom, this stuff is burning my mouth!" Emily screamed, grabbing at her throat. Her face was turning red.

"Oh lord, she ate the horseradish," Narelle's mother cried, standing and reaching for the lemonade pitcher.

"Did you eat this, honey?" Narelle said, pointing to the big dab of horseradish on Emily's plate.

Emily just kicked and gagged, her eyes watering.

"A big spoonful of it," Julian said, sound highly satisfied.

Emily kicked him, instead of her chair leg.

"Hey!" Julian shouted back.

One of the other children, whom Narelle did not know, but who was about Julian's age, sniggered. "Babies," he muttered, and ate a big mouthful of sliced beef, his cheeks rounding out.

Dylan got to his feet. "We are *not* babies! Just because it's all different here—"

"Dylan, sit down," Narelle snapped. She pushed the lemonade her mother had poured into Emily's hand. "Drink this."

Dylan sat, looking pissed.

Narelle returned to her seat. "I'm sorry," she apologized to everyone. "I think we're all still jet lagged. It's a long flight."

"Nineteen years long," Jenny said.

Narelle stared at her, astonished and hurt.

Jenny shrugged.

"I think Jenny means, my dear—" her mother began.

"You don't have to explain it to her, Vera," Joe said, sawing at his ham.

Her mother subsided.

Narelle picked up her knife and fork, but she couldn't imagine eating a single bite. All her attention, all her soul, was being pulled toward the middle of the table, where Dane sat.

Defeated, she put her knife and fork down.

"What, too weird for you, too?" Jenny asked.

"Why are you suddenly so angry?" Narelle demanded.

Jenny put her own utensils down. "Because Dane's been back an hour and you're *still* sitting yards apart, is why. You're both being stupid."

All the little side conversations around the table halted. Heads turned toward the top of the table, where Narelle sat to the right of her father.

Narelle couldn't help but glance at Dane. The urbane, unrevealing expression he'd worn since he'd come back from his ride in the rain had fled. Thunder was in his eyes, although he said nothing.

Narelle couldn't think of what to say, either.

The silence urged Jenny to continue. She sat back, her champagne glass in hand, her meal forgotten. "Lemme tell you what *really* happened when you left for America—"

Dane's chair feet squealed as he rose to his feet, pushing it back. "Jenny, *shut up*."

"No!" Jenny shot back. She thumped her glass back on the table, the contents sloshing. "There's been way too much shutting up. Nineteen years of it! And I'm *sick* of it." She jumped to her feet, too. "I love you like a brother, Dane, which means I want to shake the living shit out of you. This stoic silence of yours is killing you. *And* her." Jenny's shaking hand was pointing at Narelle.

Narelle shrank back into her chair as Dane's gaze shifted to her, then away again. His throat worked. "Talking it out won't solve anything."

"How would you know if you don't *talk it out?*" Jenny cried. She spun to face Narelle and staggered a little. For the first time Narelle wondered just how much Jenny had drunk.

"Samantha talked Dane into leaving you," Jenny declared.

Narelle gasped.

Jenny nodded, her expression grim. Her eyes were just a little bit unfocused. "She talked and talked and *talked*, until Dane didn't know if he was coming or going. She said you'd outgrow him, with that amazing job you'd got in the city. That you'd find a man in the Big Smoke and forget all about him. Said it'd be better if he dumped you before the wedding. Lots less mess." Jenny sat down abruptly.

Narelle couldn't look at Dane. It was hard enough to meet the gazes of anyone at the table. Their expressions were drawn, their eyes troubled. Her children…oh, dear sweet lord, her kids were listening to this.

Dylan, though, merely looked interested. No dismay or horror showed on his face.

Dane was still on his feet. He dropped the napkin on the table by his barely touched plate, turned and moved down the verandah to the back steps. He took the steps two at a time, strode around the house and out of sight.

And still no one said anything.

Jenny swayed toward Narelle. "*This* time, go after him, sis."

Narelle let out a shaky breath. Her gaze came back to Dylan. Her kids needed her. She couldn't leave.

Only Dylan jerked his head to one side in a gesture that was as clear as text. *Go after him!*

Narelle looked at Emily. Her daughter was no longer red in the face. She nodded.

Slowly, her heart trying to rip its way out of her chest, Narelle got to her feet. "Will you all please excuse me for a moment? Thank you." She dropped her napkin on the chair and moved down the verandah to the same stairs Dane had used, and followed the direction he had taken around the house.

Behind her, she heard heavy exhalation and a nervous titter. Forks and knives against china. They were returning to their meal.

The area in front of the house featured the single tree growing on the property. The eucalyptus tree managed to hang onto life thanks to run off from the kitchen and bathrooms. It was a huge thing which spread long shadows in the late afternoon sun.

Dane stood by the tree, his back to her, one arm thrust out to prop himself up, his hand splayed against the gnarled trunk.

He turned as Narelle came closer. His eyes were filled with pain, making her halt six feet from him. "This is not what I intended," he ground out.

"What wasn't? Jenny getting drunk? Me coming back home? What?" She raised a hand. "No, wait. I remember. You want me gone."

"Yes!" He closed his eyes for a moment, hiding the agony there. "No," he said, his voice hoarse.

"Dane, please… Jenny is drunk, but she's also right. We need to talk this out. For once, could you please use words? It's been so long, and I never did learn how to mind read."

His gaze skittered to meet hers. "You like watching me writhe with guilt?"

"Is that what you're doing?" She was genuinely puzzled. "You just seem…angry."

"For heaven's sake! I left you the day before we were supposed to get married!" He threw out his hand.

"You were gaslighted into it—that is, if Jenny is right about Samantha."

Dane stared at her. "That's…not what I thought you'd say." He blew out a breath.

Narelle shook her head. "We're both guilty, Dane. I went to the city and took the job and three weeks later, when they asked me to transfer to New York, I didn't even hesitate to say yes."

Dane rubbed the back of his neck. "I never did understand how you pulled that off. Girl from the back of beyond, in New York City. I thought you'd be terrified."

"I was," Narelle admitted. "But I was also angry. Anger got me through it. I gutted it out. I met Eddie a month after I got there and…"

Her courage ran out. "And you know the rest."

Dane turned and leaned a shoulder against the gum tree. He folded his arms and contemplated the flat horizon, where the sun was close to touching it. "I heard about the wedding. First time I've ever got drunk on scotch." He grimaced.

"I heard you got married not long after, too."

"Didn't seem to be any reason not to," Dane replied. He glanced at her and away again. "Turned out, Samantha couldn't have children."

Narelle sighed. It was a shaky sound.

"Then she got stomach cancer," Dane added. He gazed at the ochre dirt and spinifex dotting the land to the horizon. "Sam believed in her heart that she got it because of what she did to us. She told me everything, the day before she passed."

"That's how you found out," Narelle breathed. Samantha had died four years ago, two years before Narelle learned that Eddie wasn't the man she thought him to be.

"Such a waste of time," Dane muttered, his voice strained.

"No, it wasn't," Narelle said firmly.

He looked at her. His brow lifted, as he studied her with his narrowed eyes.

"I have four wonderful kids," Narelle said. "I wouldn't give them up for anyone. Dylan told me to come and speak to you, you know."

"Did he?" Dane scratched the underside of his chin, the whiskers there rasping. "He's a good kid. I talked to him…well, all of them. At the beach."

Narelle hadn't known that. "Dylan is just old enough to have opinions. Strong ones."

"Like his mother," Dane said, the corner of his mouth lifting.

"Yes." Narelle took a step closer. "The woman you walked out on was weak and stupid, Dane. She was afraid of her own shadow. If I hadn't gone to New York, if I hadn't done what terrified me, if Eddie hadn't been the asshole he turned out to be…then I wouldn't have learned how strong I really can be. I wouldn't have had the guts to come back here for Christmas and look you in the eye."

She met his gaze.

Dane didn't look away this time. Heat surged between them.

Narelle swallowed. "I didn't know what Samantha did. I didn't know why you had left. I had to come back home for the holidays to find out. And I'm glad I did."

"You should be angry," Dane said, his voice very low.

"There's no point in being angry." She moved closer, until a slight sway would press her up against him. She looked up into his eyes. "I love you, Dane. Still. Always. And I think…no, I know you love me, still. Too." She put her hands on his chest, and heard his breath catch. The heat from his skin warmed her palms through the soft shirt. "I'm not the woman you once asked to marry, but I love you anyway. Can we…is there a way we can figure things out between us?"

Dane moved very slowly. He brought his arms around her one at a time. The weight of them against her waist pulled her in against him. He gazed into her eyes. "You mean, how a New York best-selling author can take up with a station hand and live to tell the tale?"

She smoothed her hands over his chest. Let her fingertips slide over his flesh between the shirt fronts. "That's the thing about writers, Dane. We can work from anywhere, these days."

He didn't kiss her, the way she wanted him to. "Seems to me, it was your big fancy job that started the trouble in the first place." His lips grazed her cheekbone, making her nerves fizz.

She shook her head. "No, it wasn't the job, Dane. It was because we didn't work together to figure things out. I was too timid to talk about something that might threaten us, and you *never* talk."

The expression in his eyes was sober. "What are your kids going to think, about moving here?"

"They'll have a cow," Narelle said. "But they'll adjust." She gripped the front of his shirt and shook him. "We'll work it out," she said firmly. Then, hesitantly, she added, "Won't we?"

Dane pressed his lips to hers. "We will," he breathed, and *finally*, he kissed her.

Tracy Cooper-Posey is a #1 Best Selling Author. She writes historical fiction and romance of all types. She has published over 120 books since 1999, been nominated for five CAPAs including Favourite Author, and won the Emma Darcy Award.

She turned to indie publishing in 2011. Her indie titles have been nominated four times for Book Of The Year. Tracy won the award in 2012, and a SFR Galaxy Award in 2016 for "Most Intriguing Philosophical/ Social Science Questions in Galaxybuilding" She has been a national magazine editor and for a decade she taught genre fiction writing at MacEwan University.

She is addicted to Irish Breakfast tea and chocolate, sometimes taken together. In her spare time she enjoys history, Sherlock Holmes, science fiction and ignoring her treadmill. An Australian Canadian, she lives in Edmonton, Canada with her husband, a former professional wrestler, where she moved in 1996 after meeting him on-line.

Visit Tracy's site: www.tracycooperposey.com

Did you enjoy this book?

How to make a big difference!

Reviews are *powerful.*

Honest reviews help bring books to the attention of other readers. If you enjoyed this anthology, we would be grateful if you could spend just a few minutes leaving a review (it can be as short as you like) on the book's page where you bought it.

Thank you so much!

Other SRP Anthologies

Previously Released:

Space Opera Digest 2021: Fight or Flight

Stories Rule Press will be releasing genre-theme anthologies every quarter. Watch www.storiesrulepress.com/ stories-rule-press-presents for news of upcoming titles.

www.ingramcontent.com/pod-product-compliance
Lightning Source LLC
LaVergne TN
LVHW020628100826
845148LV00012B/2095

* 9 7 8 1 7 7 4 3 8 4 4 0 4 *